1 9 8 4

THE GRAYWOLF SHORT FICTION SERIES

Mercè Rodoreda

MY CHRISTINA

& Other Stories

TRANSLATED

AND WITH AN INTRODUCTION BY

DAVID H. ROSENTHAL

GRAYWOLF PRESS

PORT TOWNSEND, WASHINGTON

1984

The stories in this volume are translated from Mercè Rodoreda's original Catalan volume, *La meve Christina i altres contes*,
with the addition of one story from her book *Semblava de Sede*.

Stories in this volume have appeared in *Exile, Handbook,
Ikon, Mulch,* and *Two Tales by Mercè Rodoreda* (New York:
Red Ozier Press, 1983).

ISBN 0-915308-64-9
ISBN 0-915308-65-7 (paperback)
L C Number 84-81629

First Printing, 1984
2 3 4 5 6 7 8 9

Publication of this volume has been made possible in part
by a grant from the National Endowment for the Arts.

Designed by Tree Swenson
Typeset by Irish Setter in Palatino
Cover and frontispiece art by Frederic Amat,
courtesy of Mary-Anne Martin/Fine Art

Published by Graywolf Press, Post Office Box 142,
Port Townsend, Washington 98368. All rights reserved.

The Graywolf Short Fiction Series

Contents

Translator's Foreword

MERCÈ RODOREDA, the greatest contemporary Catalan novelist and possibly the best Mediterranean woman author since Sappho, died of cancer in April 1983. Only one of her books has been available till now in English: *The Time of the Doves* (Taplinger), which Gabriel García Márquez called "the most beautiful novel published in Spain since the Civil War."

Rodoreda, born in 1908, came of age literarily during the Spanish Republic – a time when Catalonia was autonomous and its citizens were allowed to speak, write, and study their own language. Between 1932 and 1937 she published five novels, plus numerous shorter pieces in periodicals like *Mirador*, *La Rambla*, and *Publicitat*, and was recognized as one of the most promising young Catalan authors. With the end of the Civil War in 1939, however, this whole universe collapsed. Catalan books were burned, Catalan newspapers suppressed, and offices were hung with signs saying *no ladres, habla la lengua del imperio español* (don't bark, speak the language of the Spanish empire). Along with half a million other Spaniards,

Rodoreda was forced into exile and spent the next few years trying to avoid starvation. She eventually settled in Geneva, where she eked out a greyly anonymous survivor's existence. In an interview with the magazine *Serra d'Or*, she described her state of mind during this period:

> The prewar world seemed unreal to me, and I still haven't reconstructed it. And the time I spent! Everything burned inside, but imperceptibly it was becoming a little anachronistic. And perhaps this is what hurt most. I couldn't have written a novel if they'd beaten it out of me. I was too disconnected from everything, or maybe too terribly bound up with everything, though that might sound like a paradox. In general, literature made me feel like vomiting. I could only stand the greats: Cervantes, Shakespeare, Dostoyevsky. I'm sure I've never been as lucid as I was then, possibly because I hardly ate anything.

Rodoreda remained silent until 1959, when the publication of *Twenty-two Stories* announced her return to the literary scene. After that, she regularly produced novels and became a permanent fixture on Catalan best-seller lists (*The Time of the Doves*, now in its twenty-sixth edition, has been translated into a dozen languages and was recently made into a film). Since Franco's death, most restrictions on the use of Catalan have been lifted, and in 1979 Rodoreda came home, acclaimed as a national spokesperson and adopted as a sort of patron saint by a generation of young women writers.

My Christina and Other Stories, published in 1967, is remarkable for its range of tones and atmospheres. Each tale creates a concentrated, poetically charged world, sometimes hallucinatory as in "The Gentleman and the Moon," at other times bleakly realistic as in "The Hen." Most stories fall somewhere in between, or begin in everyday reality and end in delirium. This experience of slowly sliding into nightmare was also, of course, European history in the 1930s and 1940s. It was, in one of its variations, the experience described in the above-quoted interview. All Catalans of a certain age had it – the spectacle of a nation, a culture, a language itself suppressed and throttled, for right after the Civil War it was illegal even to speak Catalan in the street. Mercè Rodoreda, however, was not only a Catalan but a writer, and a writer cut off from his or her native language is as mute as a trumpeter without a horn. Her personal story, then, was one of a kind of death, followed, with the partial loosening of controls on Catalan, by a partial rebirth.

My Christina, however, is not explicitly *about* history. Rather, it reveals Rodoreda's extraordinary receptivity to human character and experience. There are tales of tenderness like "The Nursemaid," which is an almost-untranslatable (at least into English) explosion of diminutives, and "Love," which portrays a construction worker's shy devotion to his wife. Both these stories are humorous. Their humor comes, in part, from Rodoreda's use of her favorite form, the monologue – here a vaudeville monologue both poignant and funny. Other pieces such as "The Salamander" are more like folktales, with the storyteller gradually slipping from a literal into a supernatural context. Often Rodoreda begins with a psychologically believable situation. As the story progresses, the main character's fantasies become our obsessions, and we surrender to his or her world. The result is a sense of the ambiguity of all perception, modified by a feeling that everything, finally, is rooted in the protagonist's psyche.

Part of this ambiguity arises from the characters' lack of self-awareness. Though there is intense inner life (often projected onto external details), there is almost no communication or introspection as we think of them in the United States. Feelings, even the most violent ones, tend to choke rather than

educate, and Rodoreda's heroes and heroines are often victim-
ized by their unspoken passions.

The author's primary ambiguity, however, grows out of her
own "negative capability." She can't see or hear anything
without its taking on enormous significance. The most varied
voices jostle each other, demanding our attention – peasants,
domestic servants, sailors, aristocrats. If "The Hen" reflects
the brutality of shanty-town life, "Memory of Caux" and "The
Dolls' Room" mirror the stagnant world of the Catalan upper
classes. "A Letter" and "The Salamander," both set in farming
districts, feature heroines whose constricting roles drive them
towards black magic. What most characters have in common is
that they pass through some experience in which their ordi-
nary world becomes grotesque and terrifying. In "A Letter,"
the protagonist slowly realizes she's a witch. In "The River and
the Boat," the narrator, entranced by water, finally turns into a
fish. Metamorphosis appears in many of these tales – a metamorphosis in which our "normal" masks slip away, revealing
our inner selves.

Mercè Rodoreda's art lies partly in her ability to make this
process seem inevitable, a spontaneous eruption of the subjec-
tive into the exterior, while she also presents a sharply drawn
group of personages. She is best known as a realistic novelist,
and her eye for detail and ear for speech patterns are amply
present here. Also present is her ability to create a setting at
once physically believable and emotionally resonant. What
distinguishes this book from most of her others is that here the
realistic world appears wedded to the irrational, sinister realm
of dreams and magic:

> The bottom of my skirt had turned black. I felt the fire in my
> kidneys, and from time to time, a flame chewed at my knee. It
> seemed like the ropes that tied me were already burnt. And then
> something happened which made me grit my teeth. My arms

and legs started getting shorter, like the horns on a snail I once touched with my finger, and under my head where my neck and shoulders met, I felt something stretching and piercing me. And the fire howled and the resin bubbled . . . I saw some of the people looking at me raise their arms, and others were running and bumping into the ones who hadn't moved. And one whole side of the fire collapsed in a great shower of sparks, and when the scattered wood began burning again it seemed like someone was saying "She's a salamander." And I started walking over the burning coals, very slowly, because my tail was heavy.

To place *My Christina* and its author in their proper perspective, the American reader may find some historical background useful. Catalan is a language spoken by approximately seven million people, some of whom live in the Balearic Islands, others in a small strip of Southern France that includes Perpinyà (Perpignan), and others in Spain proper, from Alacant (Alicante) to the French border and between the Mediterranean Sea and Aragon. A Romance language, Catalan is closer to Provençal and Italian than to Castilian (the language normally called "Spanish").

The most interesting Catalan literature is of two periods: the late Middle Ages and early Renaissance, and from around 1870 to the present. The first era produced such outstanding writers as the lyric poet Ausiàs March (ca. 1397-1459) and the novelist Joanot Martorell (ca. 1410-1468), whose masterpiece *Tirant lo Blanc* was described by Cervantes as "the best book of its kind in the world." During the past century, Catalonia has produced an astonishing body of artistic work. In the visual arts, the genius of figures like Joan Miró, Salvador Dalí, Juli Gonzàlez, Antoni Tàpies and Antoni Gaudí is universally recognized. Catalan writing is of equally high quality, but the world has been slower to become aware of its virtues – partly due to a lack of good translations, and partly because of the Franco government's deliberate suppression.

Since Franco's death, Catalans have moved steadily towards self-government. They now have a bilingual government and a Statute of Autonomy. Free elections to the Catalan parliament recently took place. The study of Catalan is now obligatory in the schools, and Catalan daily newspapers, television channels, and radio stations are free to operate. Thanks to authors such as Rodoreda and the poets J. V. Foix, Salvador Espriu, and Vicent Andrés Estellés, Catalan literature has remained as vital as ever. One hopes that these writers, who have spoken so eloquently for and to their nation, will now begin to receive the recognition they deserve in the United States.

David H. Rosenthal

MY CHRISTINA

& Other Stories

The Salamander

I WALKED under the willow tree, came to the patch of water-cress, and knelt beside the pond. As usual, there were frogs all around. As soon as I got there they'd come out and bounce up to me. And when I began to comb my hair, the naughtiest ones would start touching my red skirt with the five little plaits on it, or pulling the scalloped border on my petticoats, all full of frills and tucks. And the water'd grow sadder and sadder, and the trees on the hillside slowly darken. But that day the frogs leapt into the water in one jump, and the water's mirror shattered into little pieces. And when the water was all smooth again I saw his face beside mine, like two shadows watching me from the other side. And so he wouldn't think I was frightened, I got up without a word, I began walking through the grass very calmly, and as soon as I heard him following, I looked around and stopped. Everything was quiet, and one edge of the sky was already sprinkled with stars. He'd halted a little ways off, and I didn't know what to do, but suddenly I got scared and started to run. And when I realized he was catching up with

3

me, I stopped underneath the willow with my back against the trunk. He planted himself in front of me, with his arms stretched out on both sides so I couldn't escape. And then, looking into my eyes, he pressed me against the willow and with my hair all dishevelled, between him and the willow tree, I bit my lip so I wouldn't cry out from the pain in my chest and all my bones feeling like they were about to break. He put his mouth on my neck, and it burned where he put it.

The next day the trees on the hill were already black when he came, but the grass was still warm from the sun. He held me again against the willow trunk, and put his hand flat over my eyes. And all at once I felt like I was falling asleep, and the leaves were telling me things which made sense but which I didn't understand, saying them softer and softer and slower and slower. And when I couldn't hear them anymore and my tongue was frozen with terror, I asked him, "And your wife?" And he told me, "You're my wife. Only you." My back was crushing the grass I'd hardly dared walk on when I was going to comb my hair. Just a little, to catch the smell of it breaking. Only you. Afterwards, when I opened my eyes, I saw the blond hair falling and she was bent over, looking at us blankly. And when she realized I'd seen her, she grabbed my hair and said "Witch." Very softly. But she let go of me immediately and grabbed him by his shirt collar. "Go on, go on," she said. And she led him away, pushing him as they went.

We never went back to the pond. We'd meet in stables, under haystacks, in the woods with the roots. But after that day when his wife led him away, the people in the village started looking at me like they didn't see me, and some of them would cross themselves quickly as I went by. After a while, when they saw me coming they'd go into their houses and lock the doors. I started hearing a word which followed me everywhere I went, as if the air whistled it or it came from the light and the darkness. Witch, witch, witch. The doors shut. I walked through the streets of a ghost town, and the eyes I saw between the slits in the curtains were always icy. One morning I had a lot of trouble opening my front door, which was old and cracked by the sun. They'd hung an ox's head in the middle of it, with two little green branches stuck in the eyes. I took it down. It was very heavy, and I left it on the ground since I didn't know what to do with it. The branches began to dry, and while they were drying the head began to stink and there was a swarm of milk-colored worms all around the neck on the side where they'd cut it.

Another day I found a headless pigeon, its breast red with blood, and another a sheep born dead before its time and two rat's ears. And when they stopped hanging dead animals on my door, they started to throw stones. They banged against the window and roof tiles at night, as big as fists . . . Then they had a procession. It was the beginning of winter. A windy day with scurrying clouds, and the procession went very slowly, with white and purple paper flowers. I lay on the floor, watching it through the special door I'd made for the cat. And when it was almost in front of the door, with the wind, the saint, and the banners, the cat got frightened by the torches and chants and tried to come in. And when he saw me he let out a great shriek, with his back arched like a bridge. And the procession came to a halt, and the priest gave blessing after blessing, and the altar boys sang and the wind whipped the flames on the torches, and the sexton walked up and down, and everything was a flutter of white and purple petals from the paper flowers. Finally the procession went away. And before the holy water had dried on the walls, I went out looking for him and I couldn't find him anywhere. I searched in the stables, under haystacks, in the woods with the roots – I knew it by heart. I always sat on the oldest root, which was all white and dusty

like a bone. And that night, when I sat down, I suddenly realized I had no hope left. I lived facing backwards, with him
inside me like a root in the earth. The next day they wrote
"witch" on my door with a piece of charcoal. And that night,
good and loud so I could hear them, two men said they should
have burned me when I was little, along with my mother who
used to fly around on eagle's wings when everyone was
asleep. That they should have had me burned before they
started needing me to pick garlic or tie the grain and alfalfa in
sheaves or gather grapes from the poor vines.

One evening I thought I saw him at the entrance to the
woods with the roots, but when I got closer he ran away and I
couldn't tell if it was him or my desire for him or his shadow
searching for me, lost like I was among the trees, pacing to and
fro. "Witch," they said, and left me with my pain, which
wasn't at all the kind they'd meant to give me. And I thought
of the pond and the watercress and the willow's slender
branches . . . The winter was dark and flat and leafless. Just ice
and frost and the frozen moon. I couldn't move, because to
walk around in winter is to walk in front of everybody and I
didn't want them to see me. And when spring came, with its
joyous little leaves, they built a fire in the middle of the square,
using dry wood, carefully cut.

Four men from the village came looking for me: the elders.
From inside I told them I wouldn't go with them, and then the
young ones came with their big red hands, and broke down
the door with an axe. And I screamed, because they were dragging me from my own house, and I bit one and he hit the
middle of my head with his fist, and they grabbed my arms
and legs and threw me on top of the pile like one more branch,
and they bound my arms and feet and left me with my skirt
pulled up. I turned my head. The square was full of people, the
young in front of the old, and the children off to one side with

little olive branches and new Sunday smocks. And while I was looking at the children I caught sight of him. He was standing beside his wife, who was dressed in black with her blond hair, and he had his arm around her shoulder. I turned away and closed my eyes. When I opened them again, two old men came forward with burning torches, and the boys started singing the song of the burning witch. It was a very long song, and when they'd finished it the old men said they couldn't start the fire, that I wouldn't let them light it. And then the priest came up to the boys with his bowl full of holy water, and made them wet the olive branches and throw them on top of me, and soon I was covered with little olive branches, all with tiny shoots. And a little old lady, crooked and toothless, started laughing and went away and after a while she came back with two baskets full of dry heather and told the old men to spread them on the four sides of the bonfire, and she helped them, and then the fire caught. Four columns of smoke rose, and the flames twisted upwards and it seemed like a great sigh of relief went out of the hearts of all those people. The flames rose, chasing after the smoke, and I watched everything through a red downpour. And behind that water every man, woman, and child was like a happy shadow because I was burning.

The bottom of my skirt had turned black. I felt the fire in my kidneys, and from time to time, a flame chewed at my knee. It seemed like the ropes that tied me were already burnt. And then something happened which made me grit my teeth. My arms and legs started getting shorter like the horns on a snail I once touched with my finger, and under my head where my neck and shoulders met, I felt something stretching and piercing me. And the fire howled and the resin bubbled . . . I saw some of the people looking at me raise their arms, and others were running and bumping into the ones who hadn't moved. And one whole side of the fire collapsed in a great shower of sparks, and when the scattered wood began burning again it seemed like someone was saying "She's a salamander." And I started walking over the burning coals, very slowly, because my tail was heavy.

I walked on all fours with my face against the ground. I was going towards the willow tree, rubbing against the wall, but when I got to the corner I turned my head slightly and off in the distance I saw my house, which looked like a flaming torch. There was no one in the street. I went past the stone bench, and then quickly through the house full of flames and glowing coals, towards the willow, towards the watercress, and when I was outside again I turned around because I wanted to see how the roof was burning. While I was staring at it the first drop fell, one of those hot, fat drops that give birth to toads, and then others fell, slowly at first and then faster, and soon all the water in the sky had poured down and the fire went out in a great cloud of smoke. I kept still. I couldn't see a thing, because night had fallen and the night was black and dense. I set out, wading through mud and puddles. My hands enjoyed sinking in the soft mush, but my feet grew weary behind me from getting stuck so often. I would have liked to run, but I couldn't. A clap of thunder stopped me in my tracks. Then came a bolt of lightning, and through the rocks I saw the willow. I was out of breath when I reached the pond. And when, after the mud, which is dirt from the ground, I found the slime, which is dirt from the bottom of the water, I crept into a corner, half-buried between two roots. And then three little eels came along.

At dawn, I don't know if it was the next day or some other, I climbed out slowly and saw the high mountains beneath a sky smudged with clouds. I ran through the watercress and stopped at the trunk of the willow tree. The first leaves were still inside the buds, but the buds were turning green. I didn't know which way to turn. If I didn't watch where I was going, the blades of grass would prick my eyes – and I fell asleep among those blades until the sun was high in the sky. When I woke up I caught a tiny mosquito, and then looked for worms in the grass. Finally I went back to the slime and pretended to be asleep, because the three eels immediately came up, acting very playful.

The night I decided to go to the village there was lots of moonlight. The air was full of smells and the leaves were already fluttering on all the branches. I followed the path with the rocks, very carefully because the smallest things frightened me. When I got to my house, I rested. There was nothing but ruins and nettle bushes, with spiders spinning and spinning. I went around back and stopped in front of his garden. Beside the hollyhocks, the sunflowers hung their round flowers. I followed the bramble hedge without thinking why I was doing it, as if someone were telling me "Do this, do that," and slipped under his door. The ashes in the hearth were still warm. I lay down for a while, and after running around a bit all over I settled down under the bed. So tired that I fell asleep and didn't see the sunrise.

When I woke up there were shadows on the floor, because night was already falling again, and his wife was walking back and forth with a burning candle. I saw her feet and part of her legs, thin at the bottom, swollen higher up, with white stockings. Then I saw his feet, big, with blue socks falling over his ankles. And I saw their clothing fall, and heard them sitting on the bed. Their feet were dangling, his next to hers, and one of his feet went up and a sock fell, and she took off her stockings, pulling them off with both hands, and then I heard the sheets rustling as they pulled them up. They were talking very softly, and after a while, when I'd gotten used to the darkness, the moonlight came in through the window, a window with four panes and two strips of wood that made a cross. And I crawled over to the light and placed myself right under the cross because inside myself, even though I wasn't dead, there was nothing inside me that was totally alive, and I prayed hard because I didn't know if I still was a person or only a little animal, or if I was half person and half animal. And also I prayed to know where I was, because at times I felt like I was underwater, and when I was underwater I felt like I was on the ground, and I never knew where I really was. When the moon went down they woke up, and I went back to my hiding place under the bed, and started to make myself a little nest with bits of fluff. And I spent many nights between the fluff and the cross. Sometimes I'd go outside and go up to the willow tree. When I was under the bed, I'd listen. It was just like before. "Only you," he'd say. And one night when the sheet was hanging on the floor I climbed up the sheet, holding onto the folds, and got into bed beside one of his legs. And he was as quiet as a corpse. He turned a little and his leg pressed down on top of me. I couldn't move. I breathed hard because he was crushing me, and I wiped my cheek against his leg, very carefully so as not to wake him.

But one day she did a housecleaning. I saw the white stockings and the raggedy broom, and just when I least expected it blond hair was dragging on the floor and she shoved the broom under the bed. I had to run because it seemed like the broom was searching for me, and suddenly I heard a scream and saw her feet running towards the door. She came back with a burning torch and jammed half her body under the bed and tried to burn my eyes. And I, clumsy, didn't know which way to run and was dazzled and bumped into everything: the legs on the bed, the walls, the feet on the chairs. I don't know how, I found myself outside and made for the puddle of water under the horses' drinking trough, and the water covered me up but two boys saw me and went to look for reeds and started poking me. I turned and faced them, with my whole head out of the water, and stared right at them. They threw down the reeds and ran away, but immediately they came back with six or seven bigger boys, and they all threw stones and handfuls of dirt at me. A stone hit one of my little hands and broke it, but in the midst of badly aimed stones and in utter terror I was able to get away and run into the stable. And she came looking for me there with the broom, with the children constantly shouting, waiting at the door, and she poked me and tried to make me come out of my corner full of straw and I was dazzled again and bumped into the pails, the baskets, the sacks of carob beans, the horses' hoofs, and a horse reared because I'd bumped into one of his hoofs, and I went up with him. A whack from the broom touched my broken hand and almost pulled it off, and a trickle of black spit oozed from one side of my mouth. But I still was able to get away through a crack, and as I escaped I heard the broom poking and poking.

In the dead of night I went to the woods with the roots. I came out from under some bushes in the light of the rising moon. Everything seemed hopeless. The broken hand didn't hurt, but it was dangling by a sinew, and I had to lift my arm so it wouldn't drag too much. I walked a little crookedly, now over a root, now over a stone, till I got to the root where I used to sit sometimes before they dragged me off to the bonfire in the square, and I couldn't get to the other side because I kept slipping. And on and on and on, towards the willow tree, and towards the watercress and towards my slimy home under the water. The grass rustled in the wind, which whipped up bits of

dry leaves and carried off short, bright strands from the flowers beside the path. I rubbed one side of my head against a tree
trunk and slowly went towards the pond, and entered it holding my weary arm up, with the broken hand on it.

Under the water streaked with moonlight, I saw the three
eels coming. They seemed a little blurred, and intertwined
with each other, winding in and out, making slippery knots till
the littlest one came up to me and bit my broken hand. A little
juice came out of the wrist, looking like a wisp of smoke beneath the water. The eel held onto the hand and slowly pulled
it, and while he was pulling, he kept looking at me. And when
he thought I wasn't watching he gave one or two hard, stub-
born jerks. And the others played at entwining as if they were
making a rope, and the one who was biting my hand gave a
furious yank and the sinew must have snapped because he
carried off the hand and when he had it he looked at me as if to
say: "Now I've got it!" I closed my eyes for a while, and when I
opened them the eel was still there, between the shadow and
the shimmering bits of light, with the little hand in his mouth –
a sheaf of bones stuck together, covered by a bit of black skin.
And I don't know why, but all of a sudden I saw the path with
the stones, the spiders inside my house, the legs hanging over
the side of the bed. They were dangling, white and blue, like
they were sitting on top of the water, but empty, like spread-
out washing, and the rocking water made them sway from
side to side. And I saw myself under that cross made of shadows, above that fire full of colors that rose shrieking and didn't
burn me . . . And while I was seeing all these things the eels
were playing with that piece of me, letting it go and then grab-
bing it again, and the hand went from one eel to the next,
whirling around like a little leaf, with all the fingers separated.
And I was in both worlds: in the slime with the eels, and a little

in that world of I don't know where . . . till the eels got tired and the slime sucked my hand under . . . a dead shadow, slowly smoothing the dirt in the water, for days and days and days, in that slimy corner, among thirsty grass roots and willow roots that had drunk there since the beginning of time.

The Nursemaid

. . . COME HERE, little snaily snippet of lizard tail! Laugh! Go on! Laugh! Silly little creature, show me your toothies . . . Let's see. One, two, three . . . and a half! Coming down from the gummywum. Lift your arms, lift . . . You know what the ladies are doing? They're sitting in the parlor eating cakes and they're all saying "My husband, my husband . . ." while you and I have fun, shittypants, worse than shittypants. Let's see your tummy . . . plump as a little pigeon, a wee rabbit, a new-born baby partridge, a chickee-wickee, a tiny turtle, an itsy bitsy blackbird, a disgusting little pissypants . . . Lift up your armees. Say "housefly, housefly, housefly . . ." Buuum! Look at the garden. Put your arm around my neck . . . Like this, see? A nice silk scarfy. See the drizzle coming down? Look at that shiny tree, and the drops on the bellies of those leaves, drip-ping down so the lovely wormies and butterflies can get fat. Hear how they never stop talking? Those-are-the-ladies . . . Adelina, teach the girl to say papa and mama. If you sit in front of her and say pa-pa, ma-ma very slowly, so she can see how you move your lips ... That's how you teach them, little by little, small children are excellent imitators ... The child must learn to say papa before my husband's Saint's Day ... Say nitwit! Nit-wit, nit-wit ... See the little swallow, see the greenyfinch, see the blackbirdie running with three worms in his beak ... look, look ... here comes another lady, you see? Neus is going with a red umbrella to open the gate and they're saying something to each other and now she'll eat cream puffs with a little golden fork and her pinky raised, and soon I'll warm up your milk, just as white as a lily. Aren't we happy by ourselves? Shall we open the balcony door? Be brave like a lady, put your footsies in the little puddle. You like it? It's cool, it comes from heaven, the man with the beard makes it fall, who lives up there above everything, with his pants and his cap made of clouds, and he says amen. Play patty-cake ... don't you know how? Aren't you just the smallest most delightful little girl ever made? You are? And you're my little girl and we love each other? Now into your crib. I'll dry your footsies with the yellow towel ... nice and dry. So we won't catch cold and get a runny nosy. What's in your hand? A hair? Don't do that, it's naughty. Mustn't pull your hair out. It's dirty, you hear? And your hands must always be like coral ... Little witch! If the boogie man comes he'll eat you up. First one toey-woey, then another, then your footsies and kneesies ... and your little sparrow tummy. Yes indeed, don't wrinkle your nose at me. He'll have you for tea and throw away your bones, to make the glowworms laugh. Indeed he would. So you be good. Say ... pa-pa, ma-ma ... Now one of the ladies is leaving, with her hair curled and a girdle, and you look prettier with your hair all messed up like a toilet brush. Say nitwit! Nit-wit, nit-wit ... You must know how to say nitwit by your father's Saint's Day. Shall we go back out on the balcony? Come . . . you feel a little sick to your stomach? Don't you know up from down? . . . I'll make you a little clown suit and we'll go to the fair and we'll laugh and dance . . . You'll go dressed as a clown . . .

A Letter

Dear Doctor:

Don't be surprised that I describe my condition in writing. Don't be surprised that the name I sign isn't mine. I shouldn't even tell you not to be surprised, since if I didn't tell you the name at the bottom isn't mine you'd never think of it. But I must tell you, though I'm not quite sure why, that it's not mine. In a way I'm very shy, and people frighten me. These past two years I've been as giddy as a hen. Maybe if you think about it calmly, you'll figure out who I am, but as for me, if there's no cure for my disease, I'd rather you didn't think about it and didn't figure it out. Now if you do find out, in front of people I would always – since if you do find out everyone'll know – I'll always deny it. So go ahead and search.

It's hard for me to write, because farm work doesn't go very well with paper and pen, but what's been happening to me is so pent-up inside and I'm turning into such a madwoman that I have to try and explain myself in writing. Please leave a letter in the hole in that olive tree, the one on the right as you go to

17

your oldest daughter's farmhouse. If you think you can cure me, I'll come and see you. I haven't told anyone about my sickness; you're the first person to find out.

I can't remember ever being sick. I was always as strong as a horse. I can get up at the crack of dawn and work till sundown. Not now – before. Two years ago. In two years everything's changed. It all started when my husband died. But at that time I didn't realize it.

You know those late-summer dawns as well as I do. Still pale and wide-awake, perfectly silent. The wheat doesn't sway any more because it's been harvested, and the poppies – who knows where they end! One morning like that, my husband said he wanted figs for breakfast. We'd quarreled a week earlier over the interest, and I was still mad at him. "I'm going to pick some figs," he said. The leaves on the fig tree were already big and yellow and the figs were sweet like honey – especially the ones the birds had pecked at a little. I was watching him from the kitchen window while I got the chicken feed ready, and when he was looking for the ladder on the porch I thought: "You'll never make it."

He put down the basket before coming onto the porch. When he left he picked it up with one hand. In his other hand he took the ladder, and was dragging it along. You could tell he was starting to get old. I'm not sure how you could tell. Maybe because it was so hard for him to lift his feet off the ground when he walked, as if his knees wouldn't go along with the game . . . maybe because he hung his head and the back of his neck had started bulging . . . I don't know. Maybe because he was almost always in a bad mood. He climbed the ladder slowly. The basket, hung over his arm, swung from side to side, and once it caught on one of the rungs. When we were still courting, and he only worked during the wheat and grape-harvesting seasons and I first started to like him (I was the rich one and he the poor), as soon as I saw him, instead of waiting quietly to say "Good morning," I'd start shaking. The shaking would begin in my hands and move down into my legs and then up to my lips. I'd hide behind the trunk of the fig tree, and not come out till he'd passed. When the work season ended and everyone drifted away, my sisters would make fun of me: "You'll never see him again!" I still don't really know how we got married. I have to confess that after a year of marriage I was still a virgin. And what screams it cost me.

The sky, seen through the fig tree's leaves and up above it, was light purple that morning. "The figs should be cool," I thought. And I shuddered all over and shivers ran down my spine like spiders. And when I stopped looking at that glorious day, I saw my husband all the way at the top of the fig tree, like some huge bird, and I thought: "He's crazy to go so high . . ." Then the branch went "Crack!" and my husband, the basket, and some figs were all lying on the ground. The hired hand and our oldest son went to pick him up, and laid him on his bed. He was already dead. The doctor (the one we had before you, a very good person), gave me some words of consolation and even came to the burial.

Imagine a widow with sons who were still young, and all that land to take care of . . . But don't think I wasn't used to it. My husband was a gentle soul. "You wear the pants around here," my oldest son would tell me. Me, the one who wears the pants? By necessity, doctor, not by choice. And all together, we had good luck. My husband was a softy. He only yelled when he was wrong, which he always was. It's always the calm one who gives the orders, and who comes out on top. I'd let him yell. While he was yelling, I'd be thinking about what we had to do and making sure it got done. Go ahead, yell. When you've yelled awhile you won't even remember what you're yelling about, and you'll be yelling just to hear the sound of your own voice. Don't you find that when you argue with your wife, if you ever have arguments, both of you end up not knowing what you're arguing about, and you're arguing about things that have nothing to do with what started the quarrel in the first place?

I don't want to waste too much of your time. One day Miquel, my oldest son who was married, wrote to me and said he wanted to have a talk, and would I come and spend a few days at his house. At the time, I didn't want to talk about the things he wanted to discuss, so I wrote back: "I'll come later. I can't right now because for three days I've been sick in bed. I've got a very bad cold." Obviously it wasn't true, but I needed an excuse. I mailed the letter and a little while later, maybe even within half an hour, I got an awful migraine headache, I began to sneeze, my throat started itching terribly, and I had to get right into bed. The next day I couldn't get up, because I had a whopper of a cold. I know you'll say this is all old wives' tales, that my husband died because he had to die and I caught a cold because I had to catch it. But wait till the end before deciding.

I spent the next few months peacefully, just taken up with comings and goings in the house and fields . . . But one day . . . I was coming back from the market, alone in the wagon. I didn't even have to guide the horse, since he's very old and knows the way by heart. It was very cloudy. A sky full of low-lying clouds, thick, almost black in the west. I was eager to get home and fix myself a nice early supper. The path went between two dry, cracked fields. Just a little ways off to the right, there was an old, bare tree, with its branches full of ravens. The ravens came and went. Three or four would push off from the tree, flying unevenly, and then they'd return. I thought: "Everything feels dead. If the ravens would stay put, everything would feel dead." The horse stopped, and my voice died in my throat. I couldn't say "Giddyup," and the ravens in the tree and in the air froze, some on branches and others in the sky. All I could feel was this enormous fear, deep inside me. I wondered what was going on. I don't know how long I stayed like this, dead on the wagon with the horse dead and everything around me frozen. And I would have gone on this way for the rest of my life if I hadn't happened to think: "Let them fly!" The ravens on the tree, first one and then another, started taking off from the branches, the ones in the sky scattered, and the horse started walking. After a while, if I thought about what had happened while I was falling asleep, I'd get goose bumps and my heart would freeze. But that's nothing. Wait.

The day after Christmas, or actually, St. Stephen's Day, when it was already a month since the afternoon with the ravens, I went into the dining room and started a fire in the hearth. The hired hands had gone out to the stable, and the girls had gone with Agustina to clean the chicken coops and change the straw in the incubators. It was still pitch dark outside, and all you could see was the light in the stable windows, and the crack where the door to the chicken coop was half open. I got the urge to make myself some toast. I rubbed the slice of bread with a garlic clove, sprinkled a little salt on top, and then added some oil. The oil was sluggish, and I had to leave the bottle near the fire for a moment. The flames climbed the chimney in a rush of colors like I'd never seen before. The red and blue played about, coming together and separating, and the crackling wood made it look like Midsummer Night. I sat down near the fire, and when I was about to bite into the slice of bread I looked at it and thought: "It didn't get very toasted." The highest and reddest flame bent towards me, as if a gust of wind had doubled it over. It was split at the end like they'd cut it with a knife. It calmly moved closer to the slice of bread, and with great care, so as not to burn my fingertips, toasted it just right and went back to the mother flame. Then it gave a little squeal, and happily went up the chimney. What do you say to that?

One rather dull night, I was thinking what a shame it was to be a widow at such a young age. I was lying down looking at the ceiling. I had the window open, and the starlight came in, mixed with the smell of straw, leaves, and summer. I was stroking my belly, thinking how it had been full three times – full, taut, and shiny – and how when my belly was full my face would always glow. When I think about it, those quarrels with my husband weren't so important, since our bad moods always went away in bed. And look, you can believe it or not. I didn't dare to look, but without looking I saw that the sheet beside me was rising, as if someone had gotten into bed. And I felt this hand stroking my belly, a hand which wasn't mine. In the middle of the morning they found me on the floor beside the bed, unconscious. I was as pale as a magnolia, and I'd developed a nervous twitch which made one of my eyes keep blinking.

My daughter-in-law had to stop working. It was her first baby. They had a restaurant in Tossa, and there was plenty to do. As soon as the child was born, a fine, healthy-looking girl, they put her in a separate bedroom on the same side as mine – that is, between her parents' room and mine. The walls were painted pink, with a garland of pansies all around. There was a chest of drawers, a cradle that had a cover with little flowers and frills around the edges, a little table against the window with a cushion on top where you could put the girl to dress her and undress her, two chairs, and right next to the cradle, a big armchair. I'd take my afternoon nap in that armchair. One day there was a storm . . . The girl slept restlessly. She wiggled her arms and whimpered from time to time. Outside it was thundering and raining. The kind of thunder that seems like the end of the world. The water beat against the windowpanes like they were tossing it down in buckets. The shutters were closed and the light was very pale. On top of the chest of drawers, between two vases, there was a photo of my son when he was little.

I had my head on the back of the armchair, and I was thinking about things. Things from then and before, things from nowhere. I don't even know what I was thinking. The rain distracted me. But I saw bits of my life, of my children's lives, bits of everything. I jumped from one year to another, from the time of one day to the same time another day. I looked at the photo of my son, and in the midst of the darkness it seem like he was raising his arm. But just then the girl whimpered in her cradle, and I couldn't be absolutely sure. I remember there was a bolt of lightning . . . what a lightning bolt! It must have swept across the roof. And I crouched down, expecting the thunder. I remembered how the boy, when he was little, would come running up to me when he heard the thunder and clutch my skirts. And all of a sudden the thunder broke, one of those claps that came a bit after the lightning, but then they crawl through the sky like wounded beasts. And then from the deepest shadows, a little boy emerged, and just as he was clutching my skirts, my daughter-in-law came in. The boy disappeared but she saw it. "What's that kid doing here?" I told her she was seeing things. She believed it; and by the time I'd convinced her, I believed it too.

And now comes the biggest thing. I like the sea. My last days in Tossa I'd go out after supper, once everything was in order, and walk along the beach. I'd go to Codolar to watch the waves. That evening, the evening I want to talk about, the waves . . . I don't quite know how to put it . . . they were humble. I lay down on the sand. It was a hot, still night. I guess I fell asleep. When I shut my eyes to rest, everything was black, but later as I was waking up the moonlight came through the slits in my eyelids, which were just slightly open. A moon . . . as if God in person had just placed it forever between the sea and the night. As if it were made from all the blossoms on my orchard's apple trees. I looked and listened, half-asleep, and it seemed like the world was seeing with my eyes, and feeling with my senses. As if I weren't made of flesh or as if the world was me. And almost without thinking, words would come to me: blossoms, apple trees, apple trees dressed in white, white of blossoms, white blossoms of apple trees, blossoms scattered on the ground . . . And I thought how beautiful it would be to see an apple tree in the middle of the sea.

Suddenly the waves stopped, and my heart began to pound. As if when the sea's waves stopped, the waves of blood in my heart began to move. Gradually I half sat up, with one elbow stuck in the sand and my eyes round as marbles, because, doctor, a little beneath the surface the water began to make little bubbles. "Glook, glook," they went, "glook, glook." They played at being born and dying, and from the gash they left on the smooth water came flowers and more flowers. And finally, all together, they started to form an apple tree. Imagine, an apple tree in bloom at the height of summer, and in the sea. If I told you I felt feverish, I'd be telling the truth. I didn't think anything . . . I just looked, and without knowing what I was doing, I got up and went down to the edge of the water.

The apple tree was there, resting on the flat, smooth water, and I went closer to it, closer . . . There was silk on the bottoms of my feet. The water was silk. And the apple tree waited for me, as if it were saying "Come, come." When I was near it I stretched out my arm. The flowers, without there being a breath of air, drooped, sighed, were alive, were real. Before I could touch one, I, the apple tree, and the flowers all started sinking, and if I hadn't had time to call out and my son hadn't gotten worried and come looking for me, because it was hours since I'd left the house, I wouldn't be here to tell you about it, since I'm from the mountains and I never did learn how to swim.

I've had them in all colors. I'm only telling you about a few. If I had to tell you about all of them, I'd never finish. The cross I bear is that I don't dare to think. I live with constant fear in my heart. I'd like to tie a rope around my thoughts and strangle them, or else find someone like you who might believe me, and who could or would cure me. I've thought and thought about it, day and night, for many hours without stopping. And I'm scared because, after so much thinking, I feel like I finally know what's wrong with me. I think I'm a witch.

That Wall, That Mimosa

My GIRLFRIENDS laughed a lot when Miquel left me. A mania seized him for seeing the world. He said he'd come back, and they still say he will, but while they say it they're thinking I'll never see him again. And that's what I think too. Because Miquel . . . right away he wanted to sleep with me, and I really wasn't in the mood. I just wanted to go out together. I didn't know how to say no, because he told me if I didn't he'd really go astray. Maybe he'll come back someday, and if he does I wouldn't take him as a gift. Not even if they gold-plated him.

What my girlfriends all want to know is why I'm so happy when I have a cold. Let them wonder. They're surprised how I sing when I'm coughing like a dog and my nose is running like a drainpipe. I never told them how much I like soldiers, and how I fall in love when I see one. It hurts me to see them with those heavy shoes and those jackets. They wear such heavy clothes. They even do their exercises in them, out in the heat. But some of them when they cock their helmets a little over one eye . . . When they go around in threes and walk by and say

things to the girls they pass, because they're homesick.
They're like uprooted plants. The ones from the villages are so
homesick when they get here! They're homesick for their
mothers, their way of life, their normal food. They're homesick for the girls who go to the fountain and they long for everything. And with those heavy clothes to top it all off.

The three of them passed me when I was out for a walk. I
was wearing a pink frock with a little shawl tied at the neck in
that same pink, because I'd had some fabric left over. And a
tortoise-shell barrette with an imitation gold ring, that caught
my hair in a wave. The three of them stopped in front of me
and blocked my way. One who had a very round face asked me
if I had a streetcar ticket and if I'd sell it to him. I told him I
didn't have any streetcar tickets, and the other soldier said,
"Not even an old one?" And they looked at each other and
laughed, but the one who'd stayed off to one side didn't say a
thing. He had a freckle on the top of his cheek, and another
little one on his neck, near the ear. They were both the same
color: dark earth.

The two who'd wanted a streetcar ticket asked me what my
name was, and I told them straight out, since I had nothing to
hide . . . I said "Crisantema," and they said I was an autumn
flower, and how strange it was – that I, so young, could be an
autumn flower. The soldier who hadn't spoken yet said
"Come on, let's go," and the others said wait a minute, so
Crisantema can tell us what she does on weekends. And finally, just when I was feeling comfortable, they walked away
laughing and the one who hadn't said anything came up beside me. He'd left his buddies. He said he'd like very much to
see me again, because I reminded him of a girl from his village
named Jacinta . . . "What's a good day?" he asked me. And I
said "Friday evening." That's when the masters were going to
Tarragona to meet their grandson, and I was going to watch

the house and wait for Senyora Carlota, who was coming from Valencia . . . I told him where I was working and said he should write it down, but he didn't bother since he had a good memory.

When Friday came he was already there, waiting for me in the street. And some strange indescribable thing came over me, I don't know where, maybe in my veins, maybe in my skin, I don't know, but it was something very strange, since I thought if he wanted to see me it was because he was homesick. I brought along two rolls with slices of roast meat inside them. After we'd been walking a while I asked if he was hungry. I unwrapped the rolls and gave him one. We sat down to eat on a garden wall, with branches from trees and a rosebush falling over it. I ate mine in bites, pulling on it, but he had a different way of doing it. He pinched off a bit of bread and a piece of meat with his hand, and put them in his mouth. Country people are sometimes very delicate. He ate slowly, and as I watched him eat I stopped being hungry. I couldn't finish my roll, so I gave it to him, and he ate that one too.

His name was Angel. I've always liked that name. We hardly said a word to each other that day, but we got to know each other well. And when we were coming back, a gang of boys thumbed their noses at us and yelled out: "They're going to get married, they're going to get married!" The littlest boy threw a dirt bomb at us and Angel chased him, because when he saw Angel coming after him he started to run. Angel grabbed his ear and pulled it, just a little bit, gently, to give him a scare. And said he was going to lock him in the brig, and afterwards put him in the soldiers' mess and make him peel potatoes for two straight years. That's all for the first day.

The second day we walked along that street again and stopped to talk on the wall, which had one side all caked. On

the other side there was a row of little houses, with a gate that
had windows with grills on both sides of it. And the little
houses were always shut, because the people who lived in
them spent most of their time around back, which is where the
front door and the garden are supposed to be. One time, when
we were standing at the foot of the wall, and the sky was that
dusky blue that still doesn't blur things, they lit the
streetlamps. I saw that the tree we'd seen up above was a mimosa. It was coming into bloom, and it was just lovely the
whole time it had flowers. It was a good mimosa, the kind with
a few ash-colored leaves and lots of little flowers. The branches
were all like yellow clouds. Because some of them have dark
leaves, and flowers as long as a worm, and more leaves than
flowers. In the light from the streetlamp, it seemed like the
mimosa's branches were coming from heaven.

We got used to eating before they lit the streetlamps. I always brought along two rolls with a little meat inside, and
while he was eating his slowly in little pinches I'd be dying to
kiss that freckle on his neck. One of those nights I caught a
chill, because to look pretty I'd put on a pear-colored silk
blouse. When I got home my eyes were running and my head
felt like it was about to split. The next day I went to the drugstore. My mistress made me go, because she said that was no
cold I had but the flu. The clerk at the counter had very pale
eyes, almost grey. I've never seen a snake's eyes, but I'm sure
that clerk's eyes were the kind snakes have. He said I had a
spring cold. I told him how I'd spent two hours in a silk blouse
under a mimosa. And he said "It's the pollen. Don't ever stand
under a mimosa again."

One afternoon when I was on the wall with Angel, I saw a
head on the street corner nearest us. It couldn't have been a
vision, and it wasn't a chopped-off head either. It was a young

man's head. That night, thinking about the head on the corner, staring at us till it realized I'd seen it, I felt like I knew it. I could almost have sworn it was one of those soldiers who were with Angel the first time I'd seen him, and who'd asked me for a streetcar ticket. I told Angel about it. He said it couldn't be, because they'd already finished their time and gone back to their villages.

That was the last time I saw him. I never saw him again. Lots of times I'd go back to the wall and wait for him, and finally I stopped going. But sometimes it would really hurt just to think maybe he was there . . . He never even kissed me. All he did was take my hand, and hold it for a long time under the mimosa. One day, after we'd eaten, he stared at me so long and so hard that I asked him what he was looking at. He shrugged his shoulders, as if to say "If I only knew!" I gave him a piece of my bread, and he went on looking at me for a while. My cold hung on like it was planning to stay forever. Just when it seemed better, it'd break out again. Itchy nose and sneezing, and coughing fits at night. And I was happy. Afterwards when I went to the drugstore, even if it was only to buy boric acid, the clerk would say "Watch out for that mimosa . . ." And when I get a cold now, it's like I just caught it on the wall, like I was still there.

By this time Miquel's turned my head of course, and I've promised myself to him, because a good girl has to get married. But sometimes when I was with Miquel, I'd close my hand because I felt like Angel's hand was inside it. And then open it, so he could take it out if he wanted . . . so not to force him. And when my girlfriends think I'm only living for Miquel, who's gone off to see the world, I think of Angel, who disappeared like a puff of smoke. But I don't really mind. When I think of him he's mine. There's one thing that's kind of sad though . . . they have a new clerk at the drugstore. And if I ask for a package of aspirin, the new clerk, who doesn't know me, says "Here, two and a half *pessetes*." And clack!, the cash register opens. And if I ask for some citronella he looks at me and says "Two *rals*." And clack!, the cash register opens. Then I leave, but before opening the door I stand quietly for a moment. I don't really know why. As if I'd forgotten something.

Rain

She'd just put the finishing touches on the living room.
She stepped back and stood at the door to inspect her handi-
work. She'd washed the curtains the night before and ironed
them that morning. They looked pretty, all starched. They
were cream-colored, with green dots, parted and with a ruffle
at the bottom. A green ribbon gathered them at each side.

Beneath the windows sat a divan and two grey velvet easy
chairs. On the coffee table, a blue vase with roses. The huge
Breton cabinet had just been waxed; facing it, her desk with its
books neatly arranged, its clean inkwell and spotless pink blot-
ter.

Everything had been painstakingly scrubbed, dusted, made
to look just like new.

On the hope chest, to the right of the door, a crystal decanter
of cognac and two glasses sparkled. In the tiny, dazzlingly
white kitchen, a tantalizing aroma rose from a tray of pastries.
There were six more in the refrigerator: three with custard and
three with strawberries.

Everything was ready.

Marta entered the bedroom that, along with a small bathroom, rounded out her apartment. What dress should she wear? Or would a robe be better? That blue one with the flared skirt and white flowers embroidered on the bodice and pockets? She felt so pretty, so alluring in it that she thought: "If anything happens, it'll be the robe's fault." There was also a lacy tulle blouse that she hadn't worn yet . . . At last she decided upon a brown shirtdress and a thick suede belt with gold studs. She washed her face and arms, carefully combed her hair, but put on no makeup. She chose her sheerest stockings and some suede shoes.

Perfume. A last glance over her shoulder at her reflection in the mirror and she returned to the living room. She sat down.

It was early. Barely three. Since she was worn out from fighting the dirt all morning, she'd rest until he came at four. It was the first time Albert would visit her at home . . . and she felt nervous. She got up, walked to the desk, and tried to choose a book to leave on the coffee table. Which one? Maybe Shakespeare? "O my fair warrior!" Othello says to Desdemona as he greets her in Cyprus. What more pathetically pure compliment could a soldier give his lady? Like Anthony when, before his death, he calls Cleopatra "Egypt," imbuing that single word with all her queenly grandeur. Perhaps seeing such a serious book, Albert would think: "She's a snob." Basically she didn't care, but she abandoned the notion and, without further thought, picked *Du côté de chez Swann* and left it next to the roses.

She sat down again. Leaning back against the easy chair, she felt lonely. Lonely and empty. As though her excitement at Albert's visit had melted away and nothing could replace it.

She had no financial problems. A small inheritance on her mother's side gave her just enough to live on. Her job as secre-

tary in an export firm where everyone thought well of her allowed her some comfort and even a few luxuries. She had two
or three girlfriends who loved her and on whom she could
rely: good, disinterested friends. Why did her heart insist so
fiercely on something more?

She'd been in love once before. With all the passion of
youth. Now she thought it a mistake and told herself: "With
each affair, more bitterness accumulates, and besides, you can
get pregnant." When she was twenty, a timely operation had
saved her life but left her deathly afraid.

She got up. She couldn't just sit there. She rearranged the
roses so the prettiest one faced the window.

It was raining outside. It had been cloudy all day. A stub-
born drizzle, the kind that just makes everything muddy.

"Am I in love?" she wondered as she walked to the kitchen.
She couldn't resist eating one of the pastries. The coffeepot on
the stove was still warm. She poured herself a cup and
dropped an aspirin into it. She sat down on the table to drink
it.

She liked Albert, of course. Young, at once dynamic and
easygoing, simple: an excellent companion. They hadn't
known each other long but she often felt she couldn't live
without him . . . But love, so complex and vast: could it really
be embodied in a nice young man like him? True love was
behind her: "Darling, you're the only one, my kingdom . . ." A
volcano of words and feelings. Afterwards, the taste of ashes.
He'd died far away, and she'd gotten his last letter when maybe not even his corpse existed. That letter had been like poison. A cry of longing that cut her to the quick. A single wish: to
go back. It was a cursed time. And now Albert. Very restful,
certainly . . . There was no one else around, yet how deep did it
go? One day he'd ask her to marry him and they'd rent a big
apartment. If he was faithful, he'd be demanding, severe,

gloomy. He'd grow old slowly. If he wasn't, he'd be indulgent, broad-minded, he'd have heart trouble and lock himself in a world from which she'd be excluded.

She got off the table and paced to and fro, with a cup of coffee in one hand and a second pastry in the other.

"He'll bring me a bouquet and a box of chocolates. We'll talk about the weather, politics. He'll tell me his philosophy of life but we'll both be thinking of something else. Before leaving he'll tell me how much he loves me and ask for a kiss, which I'll gladly grant him.

"Or maybe he'll storm in looking determined, a little dramatic, and he'll say: 'I can't live without you.' He'll squeeze my arms. 'You hear me? It's impossible; I can't live without you! I want you every day, every night, beside me all night long.' His eyes will glow, he'll kiss me greedily: my cheeks, neck, and lips. He'll try to unbutton my dress, to get me excited too. Yes, my breasts are pretty and a little attention wouldn't hurt . . . Maybe I'd like it too much. But I don't want to. No, it's not that I'm prudish. I've got my own ideas about many things and a certain notion of how to live, but . . ."

She went back to the bedroom. Then the bathroom. She plucked a hair from the sink. She straightened the bottle of cologne. The mirror had fogged up, so she wiped it and looked at herself.

"Why complicate your life? You feel alone? If he leaves you you'll feel even worse. They're making a dress that'll be my favorite. They're fixing an antique ring that used to be my mother's; it'll be sumptuous, maybe too much for someone as young as me. I've got ten pairs of gloves and an exquisite lingerie collection. This year my bank account has grown considerably. No one kisses me. But kisses often turn out to be costly . . ."

A churchbell rang. It was three-thirty.

She felt like running away, escaping a danger she could scarcely identify. She'd been silly to invite him. She hadn't given it much thought, but he'd be full of hopes she couldn't bring herself to share.

Determined, she put on a felt hat and raincoat and shut the door behind her. As soon as she reached the landing, she smelled the rain. She was down the stairs like a shot.

The street was deserted; on one side was row of single-storey houses, on the other, a garden. When the trees along the wall were bare, she could see a tennis court and swimming pool from her window. In spring, the fragrance from the acacias and honeysuckle made her dizzy. When she left work in the evening, she approached the street slowly, savoring that intoxicating perfume, which at night filtered through her balcony.

It was drizzling. Everything glistened: the sidewalk, the cobblestones, the grass poking between the cracks. Water trickled down the walls and drops fell from tiled roofs. The sky looked like lead, and everything was immersed in milky radiance, as if the trees and houses got their light from an airshaft.

As she started walking, she wondered where she'd go. Where did this urge to flee come from, pushing her through the streets? On a windowsill stood a kitten with a string around its neck. Every time a drop fell on its nose, it looked up. Inside she could hear children screaming.

She walked with her hands in her pockets, her hat pulled down. The streets were deserted. The air seemed still. After a while, a woman carrying milk bottles crossed her path; the bottles clanked together. She passed a nursery school; she could hear the little kids singing. As she approached the center of town, there were more people in the street. Passers-by hurrying beneath umbrellas, with their hopes and their cares. The shop windows were full and some had turned their lights on. A grocer had covered his outdoor fruit stand with a big tarpaulin.

She entered a café. The men were playing billiards and cards. Some whispered and argued, as though they were talking business.

"A coffee."

"Our machine's just gone on the blink."

"Some herb tea, then."

And it kept drizzling. Cars passed, shiny in the rain, a rattling streetcar, a wagon, its drowsy driver wearing a wet sack on his head. People entered the movie house across the street. Inside the bar, a dreamy little boy slowly collected cigarette butts. A lottery ticket vendor asked if she'd like to try her luck; she declined with a weary gesture.

What about going to the movies? But she'd already seen the film. Queen Elizabeth's green feather fan. She remembered Her Majesty's shadow as she descended a staircase. That mirror with a queen inside it ... She forgot the film. The rain reminded her of those lines by Valéry and she wondered why they were famous: whether Valéry had made them famous or the other way around.

She was beginning to feel tired. She paid and left.

It was still raining. It had been raining since early morning. No downpours; just a calm, steady drizzle. She walked beneath some trees. Their leafy branches met, creating a green, aqueous tunnel. She passed a church. The bells were striking four. Only four o'clock? Every peal stabbed her heart ... It was absurd, what she was doing. Out of character. She ought to hail a taxi and give the driver her address. But she did nothing. Something stronger than herself held her back.

She couldn't help realizing that the man loved her. Eyes don't lie, and neither do tones of voice. But she had a past. Sooner or later, she'd have to tell him she'd done something crazy. Two things: loving and preventing her child's birth. He'd be four years old by now, and she wouldn't be alone.

But no, that wasn't why she'd left. "Then what was it?" she asked herself impatiently. "Why this fear of a new love? Why this self-absorption, as if you were a crotchety old lady?"

She hurried beneath the dense foliage. She could hear her steps, her breathing, the blood throbbing in her temples. She walked rhythmically. O my fair warrior! There was a bench every hundred yards on the promenade. She felt like sitting down, calmly savoring the undersea light and the sound of rain on the leaves. A kind of modesty held her back. A phrase from she didn't know where had been floating through her mind: *And on just such a night, Queen Dido called out from Carthage to fleeing Aeneas . . . and the lion's shadow frightened him . . .* No, that wasn't right: *And on just such a night, Queen Dido with a willow branch . . .* Now it was Dido who fled. She laughed and muttered: "Idiot!" Tomorrow, seated before the typewriter: "Dear Sir: The shipment of canned sardines, scheduled for mid-September, has been delayed due to circumstances beyond our . . ."

He must have climbed the stairs. Now he was probably ringing the bell with a bouquet in his hand, smoothing his jacket with a swift, unconscious gesture, breathing heavily because he'd mounted the steps quickly. Nothing. Emptiness and silence. He rang again. He grew impatient. He rang again. Nervously. More silence. Finally, with a last glimmer of hope, he'd ring again. Till, disappointed, he'd put on his hat and descend the stairs.

And she walked on. She'd never walked down so many streets in one afternoon. Her feet were frozen, but her face was sweaty. She walked for hours. When the bells struck seven, exhausted, she entered her street. The street said nothing: neither that he'd arrived happily nor that he'd gone away sadly.

The shadow of a streetlamp cracked into pieces on the wall and a radio sent out waves of waltz music.

Against the light, she saw the slender needles of rain. The sky was opaque: it would rain all night and then some more.

She groped her way up the steps, like a reveler returning from an orgy. The staircase said no more than the street.

She entered her apartment. A wave of perfume hit her. She'd dabbed some on the easy chairs, the ribbons on the curtains, when she'd finished cleaning. It was a perfume he liked, and she'd done it to please him.

She shut the door and, with a weary gesture, threw down her hat. She left her raincoat in the kitchen. Her head ached, her tongue was white as chalk, her legs hurt.

Everything was the same; the *aubepines* in Proust's book were surely prettier than ever. Who could imagine everything that had happened that afternoon? That is, everything that hadn't happened, everything irretrievably submerged just when it was about to become real? She hardly could herself. Not even her. She knew nothing. Neither why she'd left nor why he'd come. "I can't think about what I don't know; for me it doesn't exist. China suddenly exists when I think of it, when I say: 'Flowering cherry tree, Fire dragon . . .' China or Japan . . . The Dalai Lama's dead if I think he is. The man I expected this afternoon existed because I'd met him, and I existed for him because he wanted me. God, what a headache!"

She entered her bedroom. She'd skip supper. All she wanted was to sleep. She started undressing . . . *Oui, c'est pour moi, pour moi/que je fleuris, déserte!* Now she'd have the imprints of kisses on her shoulders, her arms, her lips; she could hold onto them and they'd keep her company at night. She could slip them beneath her pillow and maybe they'd come out while she was sleeping, returning to the same spots on her arms and shoulders.

She put on her prettiest, most diaphanous, most bridal nightgown. The perfume made her head spin. She turned off the light and opened the balcony doors. The light from the streetlamp entered her room. The monotonous rain fell relentlessly. The night smelled wet. It must be cold.

Barefoot, she went to fetch the decanter of cognac. She was shivering. The bottle was cool against her fingers. "I'll get drunk," she thought. O my fair warrior!? . . . And she drank three glasses in quick succession, all full to the brim.

Memory of Caux

LISTEN, and you'll hear all about it . . . It's an adventure and it's not. I was almost twenty at the time . . . Imagine! At home I suffered . . . how shall I say . . . a nervous disorder, a *break-down*, you know? I didn't eat or sleep, all day long with the pain right here in the middle, that is, a little to one side, be-tween my heart and my stomach. Very bad. The doctor said I needed some distraction. No studying, no worry. Distraction, distraction. And for the moment, he advised me to go hunting every morning in the woods. I'd never hunted anything, you know? But the doctor said maybe hunting would be good for me.

And listen . . . the boys in the village, when they saw me coming, would call out to each other and gang up, and they followed me back to the house, laughing because I always came back with an empty bag (they didn't know I couldn't care less). A bird takes off from a tree and . . . zip, zoom, he flies this way, that way . . . and it keeps you from thinking. The village boys ended up making such a racket that sometimes I'd go all

41

the way round and come back from the side where the fields were, instead of from the woods side.

You can't imagine how much I enjoyed it. You're inside a bush, quiet, waiting ... The bird flies by, whirls around, comes back, goes away, comes back ... it seems like he might want to land on a branch, then he's flying again because he heard a twig crackle, and then, when you least expect it, click! he's sitting there. And there you have him, like a little ball of wool ... because the doctor said hunt birds, have some fun ... you've got him there and slowly, without breathing, you point the gun, take aim, and shoot ... and the bird flies off happily into the sky or the woods ...

But in the end, the doctor told my father that perhaps I'd be better off spending a few months abroad ... My father! ... Mother of God. When I was twelve I wrote a letter to a girl who was fifteen. It started like this: *Inolvidable Juanita: desde que te vi, mis ojos se fijaron en ti*. The girl passed the letter on to her father, who gave it to my father ... And whenever we had visitors, my father would send the maid to fetch me from my room, and he'd make me come into the living room and shake hands with the visitors and then, right in front of everyone, with his hands folded behind him, he made me read the letter from beginning to end ... *Inolvidable Juanita* ... etc., etc. It lasted a whole year, this joke. My father ... And he loved me, you know? My mother died when I was born, and when she entered the house as a bride she said "I want earth." (land, she meant ...)

You know Montreux? My father sent me to Montreux. To Caux, that is. You know that mountain with the hotel on top? I stayed in that hotel. Below, there was Leman, with the peaceful water and, on the other side of the lake, the mountains touching, towering over each other. The Teeth of Midday ... and I don't know how many more! I lived very peacefully there. Every morning I went horseback-riding. Afterwards I

slept, or spent hours and hours looking at the sky in one of
those folding deck chairs. I sat on the lawn and read poetry. I
ate like a king. I don't remember the entire schedule, you
know? So much time has passed . . . I was young, twenty years
old, imagine! They played the Brahms Quintet in C Minor. The
clarinet quintet! That probably doesn't mean anything to you.
But that quintet! You can't imagine the atmosphere at the con-
certs during that period. Mother of God! A colony of the
wealthy. Caux, Montreux . . . the castle of Chillon nearby, the
blood-colored ivy – because it was fall, a warm fall in which it
slowly turned to gold, blessedly calm. The hotel on top of the
mountain, with its roof touching the sky, like an eagle's eyrie.
The shadow of Byron . . . Shelley . . . and everything those
names suggest.

The concert began with a symphony by I don't know who.
And I remember the vast silence, the impeccable conductor,
the bows moving swiftly up and down –, nyigu-nyigu, nyigu-
nyigu . . . and the audience, very elegant, with some ladies . . .
Mother of God, it's better not even to mention them! And over
everything, the shadow of Isabel of Austria, assassinated a few
years earlier in Geneva. One of the loveliest women in Europe
. . . People from the embassies with their families, millionaires
from Britain and Argentina, plump and contented, or intense
with feverish eyes, truckloads of diamonds . . . And Byron!
The day, the hour, the sunshine and the shade . . . Empress Isabel
. . . Were you ever in Vienna? Really? One afternoon, in the
Prater . . . but never mind that. If you ever go to Montreux,
between Montreux and Chillon you'll see the English cemetery. At the entrance there's a statue. Something quite marvelous, with all that it suggests. A lady of extreme nobility, seated, with flowers in her hand . . . I don't know . . . marvelous.
The time I spent looking at her! . . . And the music unfolding
its magic. The Brahms quintet! *Presto non assai ma con sentimen-*

to. At times I felt like there was a delirious dove in my stomach. I had my eyes shut, and just when it seemed like I was floating in midair, I felt a drop of sweat roll down my neck. I very carefully took my handkerchief out of my pocket so I could wipe it off, and as I turned my head to get at my neck with the handkerchief, I saw her.

I don't know how to describe her. The best thing is not even to try . . . She was sitting two rows up, on the same side as the first row of violins. The only thing missing was a bouquet in her hand. The hair, the profile . . . and the face – delicate, tender, ladylike, between Reynolds and Gainsborough, you know? . . . And the music, spreading in waves through the hall. Maybe you won't believe me, but my hands shook and my heart was pounding like a churchbell. I closed my eyes again . . . I was only twenty, it's been forty years since that day, and it's like I was still there: the clarinet, ta, ta, ta, ti, ta, taTI . . . taTI, ti, ti, ti, ti, ti, ti . . . ti tiriRIT . . . tiriRIT. Of course I hope you won't laugh at me . . . I have a lot of trust in you . . . By the time they'd finished, the hall was submerged. And there were bouquets of lilies everywhere. Mother of God! The applause distracted me and the girl disappeared among the crowd . . . Like in a novel, you know?

That girl, who I thought had disappeared forever, was staying in my hotel. It was an idyll. We went horseback-riding every morning. Two indescribable months. And one fine day she left, and I hadn't the courage to declare myself . . . I didn't dare. Always weighed down by doubts. She left. By chance, a little before the end of that fall, I found out her address. She lived in the German part of Switzerland, in a convent. No, it wasn't really a convent, it was a residence run by the Protestant parish. After many doubts, I took a train and went there. I wanted to see her, to tell her . . . Don't laugh, don't, it's not a laughing matter. I was a bundle of nerves . . . And as soon as I got off the train, it occurred to me that I'd made a mistake in coming without announcing myself. At the time those things were important. I wandered through the town, looking for a place where they might sell paper and envelopes. I'd write her a brief note, so as not to surprise her. Finally, I found a little shop that had everything. And now comes the biggest thing. I was half-sick, yellow as a corpse . . . When I went into the shop I thought the words wouldn't come out of my mouth . . . I just stood there, waiting. There were some little bell jars up above with alpine flowers inside them. Very pretty. In a corner, the lady who ran the shop and another woman were sorting through some small pitchers . . . Suddenly I got uneasy, and I thought I'd gone crazy. I left without opening my mouth. Inside I was telling myself, "Don't run, whatever you do don't run . . ." Then from one winding street into another that made several turns, and a little square with a fountain in the middle, and a sort of promenade with short, thick trees . . . and there I was, lost, looking for the station, which I simply couldn't find, as if it had melted away. And when I got there it seemed like a station in a dream, and I felt like I'd saved myself from I don't know what. And I went back – all the way to Montreux. And that's how it ended, so cold it tore your skin, and me by the fireside reading poets who wrote as if they'd known her. *She walks in beauty like the night . . .*

A long time afterwards, maybe twelve years, I lived for quite a while in Paris. I've always been very fond of walking, as you know. I know Paris by heart, all the neighborhoods, all the streets, all the corners. And the cemeteries. I've spent whole afternoons wandering through the cemeteries. One evening, I think I already told you about it, they locked me in Père Lachaise . . . I had to get out through a little gate around the side. Finally, when by this time everything about that autumn seemed like a dream, I saw her one day in the street. Just like that. She was getting out of a taxi. I followed her for a moment, but she immediately went into a building. I wanted to know if she lived there, and I could have asked the concierge, but I had a friend ask for me the next day. And sure enough, she was living in Paris in that building. And she still wasn't married! What do you think of that? Everything came back to me, it was like a huge whirlwind: Montreux, Caux and the horses, the lake like a sheet of steel ... *she walks* ... *like the night* ... I confided in my friend, who knew me well, and he advised me to go see her, and to do what I hadn't done when I was twenty – to declare myself. Get dressed up and go. How should I dress? Solemn. Solemnly, you know? In a morning coat. I went in a morning coat and pinstriped pants. I bought a bouquet ... I wandered through the streets of Paris, and it was like I'd never been there before. I could have taken a cab, but I wanted to go on foot to see if I could get rid of some of my nervousness on the way ... And listen, whether you believe me or not ... walking and walking, I got lost. I started wandering round and round in circles, and me full of all those things, which after so many years were coming back with more fire and more colors ... *Herein is enshrined the soul of the clarinet* ... That music, all sighs: faaa, sol, fa, mi, fa, sol, mi, faaa ... mi, re, do, re, mi, do, ree ... la-luu ... Mother of God! Do you know I always travel with the record in my suitcase? ...

At last I managed to find the building. But I didn't go through the entrance. I couldn't. Some distance away, I sat down on a bench. I put down the flowers, making sure no one would see me, and I went home. What do you think of that? But wait, this is the horrible part. A couple of months later, I had to leave Paris, and I started travelling all over. Professional matters, you know? Years went by, and one fine day I found myself married to a Viennese ... Vienna ... let's not get into that, my God, let's not get into that ... There was a big rush, some of my relatives arranged it for me. You know my wife, my house . . . You can't imagine what luck I've had. If it hadn't been for those bridge parties! . . .

Anyway, more years passed, many more years. Everything in this story is years passing. And after many years of travelling around, my wife and I decided to settle in Paris. Paris again. And listen, to wrap it all up: at the beginning of this year, looking for the phone number of some friends who were going to Barcelona – I wanted to give them a letter for my estate manager . . . that nonsense about the field they were building a road through, you know? – I saw her name. She lives across the street . . . well, not right across, but very close, you understand? It's possible that we sometimes pass each other, and I don't know who she is and she doesn't know who I am. *Too long . . . too late.* I don't even know who she is. And I don't want to know . . . Mother of God . . . I don't even want to know.

The Hen

WHEN I THINK too long about the same thing, I get dizzy. I only feel good when I'm alone, sitting up here with my legs dangling over the side, looking out. This quarry was full of stone. Now it's closed. I work up all the saliva I can, and then I spit down onto the last pile of stone they brought up, the one the truck never came for. If my spit hits the pile, I hear it. If it misses I don't hear a thing. When the wind blows I sometimes miss. From here I can see the shacks spread out, the cat on a rooftop, and over on the right, the garbage heap. Now the dog's started barking. He always barks when night comes, like he was crying over the sunset. Our shack is the one in the middle. My father always says it was the first one built here, and the others sprang up around it. My father calls our shack the mother-hen. The trucks would come, raising dust in the summer and packing down the mud in winter. And the stone brought forth stone. Everyone said so. The stone from the mountain had three colors: grey, yellow, and rust – all a little dead. On the side with the barking dog, a cloud is coming, with one whole edge ragged like it was made of feathers. I won't go home. I'll stay and live here till the wind dries me up. There are grasses that live here till the wind shrivels them. Then it uproots some of them and carries them away.

I've been wanting to leave ever since my mother died. At night sometimes when she was still alive, my father would say "Go outside, enjoy the fresh air." And I left and he closed the door. I stood still for a minute, and then started wandering among the shacks. I enjoyed listening to the people talking inside and seeing the lights in the windows, which gave me lots of company in the dark. I went over to the garbage heap and was looking for bits of broken dishes. And sardine cans. By sticking the broken sides of the dishes in the ground, I made the paths and walls of a cemetery. The paths wouldn't stay very straight, though I tried my best. The sardine cans were the coffins. I filled them up halfway with water, and then found some ants and threw them inside. The cemetery started with just one can, and gradually expanded. After a while my father yelled for me to come. It was like an ox bellowing. In the winter no one was out. It's too cold, everything was too muddy, and I stayed just outside the door. I could hear like I was inside. If it rained, I'd come out in an old overcoat which was my bed and covered my head and sometimes my face and everything, so I wouldn't see or hear a thing. One night a man came by who knew me and without stopping said "Some joke, kid!"

My mother's name was Matilde. When she was in a bad mood she'd look at me and mutter: "I wonder why we ever had you." And when my father was late and she had to warm up his dinner, she'd pass the time saying she didn't know why we were in this world. We kept a pair of rabbits in a low cage by one side of the shack, on the wall which had no windows. Because of the stench. The wire was rusty. There were two broken sticks – I mean two legs – and my father had fixed them with a piece of wood and some tape to hold them together. In summer the stench from the rabbits came into the shack. When we ate the rabbits my mother would kill them, and I had to help her. She hit them on the back of the head with a mortar, and then while they were stunned she hung them by their legs from a big nail on one side of the entrance, and slit their throats with a knife. I held the cup while the blood ran out. Then she cut around the bottom of their legs and pulled off the skins, which she turned inside out, all wet and full of colors. If the skin wouldn't come beyond the ears, she chopped them off, and with a good pull yanked it down as far as the teeth. Then she hung the skins on the cage so they could dry out. When the skin was soft, the flies made black clusters on the white lined with bright red veins. One day when my mother was feeding the rabbits cauliflower leaves, one of them got out of the cage, like a devil she said. I didn't find it until nightfall, by the side of the shack, one of the last ones. The cat had killed it, and only half of it was left.

My mother traded the other one for a yellow hen with black feathers on the tips of its wings. Her comb hung down on one side and covered half her face. Her crop was torn. She lived peacefully inside the rabbit hutch, and during the laying season gave us an egg every day. As soon as the hen started clucking I'd go get the egg, and my mother said I should wave it in front of my eyes, that it'd be good for my vision. One day the shell was so thin that the egg broke between my fingers and the white and yolk both ended up on the ground. My mother went to look at the hen, which was pacing up and down in its cage, and said it needed some lime in its diet. On Sundays a neighbor would save the bone from her cuttlefish for us, which looked like a white boat. The hen picked at it, but soon she started laying eggs with no shells at all and finally we gave her broken shells to eat, which she enjoyed a lot. Then she went back to laying eggs with shells, but she ate all the eggs because she'd taken a liking to eggshells. My father sometimes would stand in front of the cage, looking at the hen and saying "She lives like a landlord."

When my mother got sick, I used to hear her breathing from my corner like it was right in my ear, and the neighbors said the fever was burning her up. And when she died they said the fever had been too much for her. I had to fix the meals and sweep the shack and go fetch water from the fountain. My father was in a daze and never opened his mouth. At night I heard him tossing from side to side. Then one day he called me and said "Come." So I got in beside him, and slept on the side of the mattress where my mother had made a hollow from sleeping there so many years. I had a hard time sleeping there, for two reasons: because I wasn't used to being so high up – I'd been sleeping on that old overcoat – and because the hollow place scared me and I hardly dared breathe. One night I started crying. After a long time my father woke up and asked me "What's going on?" I didn't dare tell him that the hollow was burning from my mother's fever and I felt like I was sleeping on top of her right after having killed her, and he said "Stop that crying or get out." And I went out and choked my sobs and fell asleep peacefully on the ground. The very next day my father took the hen, broke up the cage with an axe, and ate his whole dinner with the hen on his lap. She was quiet, watching everything, sometimes with both eyes and sometimes with only one, and my father gave her bits of bread to eat. Afterwards, my father sent me out for a dish of water and made her drink. Everytime she swallowed some water her head would bob up and down and my father laughed. And from that night on my father slept with the hen.

I planted six beanstalks. Three on each side of the door. My mother did it every year. On the wall, along with the nail where she'd hung the rabbits to kill them, there were wires stretched so the beans could climb. The beans began to grow. When they broke through the soil a little of it would stay on top of them like tiny hats. And when the hats fell, the hen would eat the sprouts. I planted more, and made a hedge all around them with reeds from the stream. The hen was watching me while I did it. Sometimes she came up close and sometimes kept her distance, holding up one of her lead-colored legs. The cat who'd killed the rabbit was the only cat in the shacks, and was half-wild. No one ever gave him food, to make sure he'd hunt the rats. At night he'd wander around. In the daytime he slept on the roofs. One day I caught him and shut him up in the shack with the hen. The cat's meowing and the hen's fussing were terrible. When they calmed down I opened the door. The cat dashed out and the hen jumped on top of me, smearing me with the blood gushing out of her comb.

I've done everything I could think of to get her out of the house, but nothing's worked. When my father comes home from work, he calls out "Here, here, my little one" as he comes up the path. She waits for him, they come in together, and he gives her cabbage leaves he gets from a friend at work. Last night we went out to enjoy the coolness. The beanstalks have grown and they're now in bloom. My father put the hen on his shoulder and walked around, saying to it in a soft voice, "Eat the flowers, eat them." Then he sat down and told me to get his supper, and said he wanted an onion in his salad. I didn't have any onions, so I went to borrow one from that neighbor who'd given us the cuttlefish bones when the hen was laying eggs with no shells. It was dark, and so hot you couldn't breathe. I came back, dragging my feet to make paths in the dust. From time to time, I stopped to look at the sky, because by now I was sick of everything. The sky was different from other nights, thick and low, with the kind of stars that don't shine much. Before turning the corner of our shack, I heard my father's voice, as if he was talking with someone. I couldn't catch what he said. I went a little closer and peeked around the corner. My father had the hen in his lap. He was stroking her back with his hand, saying very softly, "Matilde, Matilde . . ." The hen was like a peaceful shadow . . . I lost the urge to go home. I just want to be alone, without thinking, spitting.

Therafina

YETH MA'AM, I'm the new maid . . . I know it'th nine and I
wuth thuppothed to come at three, but I got a little lotht and
jutht when I thought I wuth there a very well-drethed man
told me I wuth in Thanth. He told me how to get to Than
Gervathi and, athking and athking, they ended up thending
me to the thoo. I thaw all the animalth: tigerth, elephanth, the
cockatooth and the monkeeth. Then I came out on the
Ramblath and I wuth thtrolling among the flowerth and the
gentlemen who were walking by thed thingth to me. One who
wuth carrying a walking-thtick invited me for a beer. I didn't
know him, but we thoon got acquainted. He told me he wuth
rich and wanted very much to get married. Don't worry, nothing happened to me. Do you live alone? Tho it really would
have thcared you if I hadn't come . . . If you knew how much
time I thpent wandering through thowth threeth . . . I wuth
thircling round the howth and I thaw the ladeeth going in, and
every time I ran up to go in with them it wuth too late. I wuth
about to jump over the wall in back, but I wuthn't sure it wuth

54

the wall to your garden . . . Why didn't I ring the doorbell? Becawth whenever I went to touch it I got thtung. When I'm a little nervuth everything I touch thtingth me like it wuth full of electrithity . . . I don't have any thootcatheth, I've got everything in thith little bundle . . . No, I'm not a bit tired, I could have made ten tripth like thith without getting tired, but if you want I'll thit down in thith nyth little armchair. You thee, I thought ath thoon ath I arrived I'd have to thtart washing disheth. If you keep me, I'll fix up your garden in the thummer, and on the wall at the bottom, tho it won't theem tho bare, I'll plant bluebellth and a pumpkin. Do you like a good pumpkin thoop? I like it, but it alwayth givth me the hiccupth . . . What wuth my life like in the village? You could thay it wuth pretty hard. Taking care of the howth and the henth and helping my mother bring up theven little brotherth and thithterth . . . And when they were grown up mother thed I'd be better off in thervith tho I could thave thumthing and thend her a few penneeth . . . Yeth ma'am, I've therved in two howtheth. I think the preetht already told you in the letter he wrote . . . In the firtht I only thtayed two weekth becawth the boy wuth very mithchevuth. Whenever we were alone he'd call out "Therafina!" The firtht day I ran up right away. He made me thtand in the middle of the hall like a peeth of wood, backed up a wayth behind me, grabbed a board, and gave me thuch a whack on the behind that without wanting to I ran five yardth, ath far ath the gallery windowth. And he yelled out: "Goal!" And he made me do thith the whole blethed afternoon. I didn't know how to thay no, becawth even though he wuth only a boy of fourteen, he wuth my mathter'th thun and I wuth the maid. In the thecond howth I wuth better off for a while, but the mathter and mithtreth were old and didn't get along well and mithtreth, who wuth thickly and thpent the dayth lying in bed, wuth thcared that her huthband would put poythun in her medithin and she told me I had to be very watchful, and wanted only me to give her the dropth and I had to count them there in front of her. They both got jealuth over me, and when one of them finished the other would take me. And both of them athked me theparately, "You like me better, don't you?" ... When it wuth the mathter who caught me he'd tell me how he'd had bad luck and married a craythy woman, and how even though the mithtreth knew he had a delicate thtumack she'd make him eat heavy meelth to make it wurth. And he wuth sure she put thulfur in the thawtheth. And when I wuth jutht getting uthd to the howth I thtarted feeling thick and after thum dayth I wondered if they'd put thumthing bad in my milk and I got tho frightened I couldn't thleep at night and the day after I hadn't thlept, when I wuth duthting the furniture my whole body felt like it wuth going to ... Am I engaged? Not now, but I have been twyth. The firtht one wuth named Miqueló. He wuth ath fair ath wheat and he died in Africa. I met him by the fountain. I wuth thtrolling beneath the acathiath and I heard thomeone thay "What a honey pie!" I turned around and I thaw a bunch of young fellowth kidding around. When I wuth jutht about to throw a rock at them they came up and told me I wuth very pretty, all of them at wunth, but my hair wuth a little methy, and the one who'd thed I looked like a honey pie had a little leaf in hith hand that he'd been playing with, and he thtuck it in my hair. From then on we alwayth thaw each other and we'd take walkth bethide the road, and one night when we were wandering among the vinyardth up above, we went into a little wooden shack. He made me take off my clowth, and told me to lie down on the floor. He lay down bethide me, lit a thigarette, and thtarted flicking the asheth in my belly-button. And when he'd thmoked the thigarette he thtarted pulling the hairth out from under my arm, tho hard it brought tearth to my eyeth. And we went to the little shack another day when it wuth raining, and the water came through in bucketth onto the floor and when we finished my whole back wuth dirty with mud and we laughed a lot. I didn't like it all that much becawth I get gooth bumpth when they touch me. When I wuth little, one time a girl who went to thkool with me infected me with her lithe, and when my mother would pick them out each morning I hated it when she touched my head. A few monthth later I had to leave the village, even though my belly couldn't be theen becawth every day my mother put a tight girdle on it. I went to thtay with an aunt who livth three hourth from my howth and I had a little girl there. Ath thoon ath she thtarted breathing she died becawth she didn't have any bownth. By thith time Miqueló wuth in Africa ... The day he went away he told me they were thending him off to the wildth of Morocco and they'd kill him there with thayberth and we'd never thee each other again, and he thed if they killed him, while he wuth dying he'd think of me ... After the thing with the girl Mr. Vidal, the druggitht'th thun, thtarted following me around. He wuth ath dark ath Miqueló wuth fair, and he looked like a gypthy. But nyther. At night he'd jump through the window and get into bed with me. And he told me thum pretty thingth ... Before thunrithe he'd get up, put on hith jacket, and run out. I'd watch him through the window and blow him a kith. And one thummer he didn't come back becawth he'd gotten engaged to a girl in Barthelona. And if I'm glad to be working in Barthelona it'th becawth I think maybe I'll find him and I'll be able to thmooth back hith bangth which always uthed to fall in hith fayth and which wuth thumthing he loved for me to do. And now you know everything. I think you'll like my work. I'm very clean and I eat like a bird. I'm never thick. The only thing that happenth ith if I don't bundle up well I catch a cold. The only thing wrong with me ith my lithp. You'll keep me, won't you?

The Dolls' Room

DEAR FATHER JOAN MAYOLS:

My name won't mean much to you, but perhaps that doesn't matter. If today I take my pen in hand, all green and a little bristly, through no carelessness of my own but because I've had it so long, and especially since I don't want to replace it with a new one, now that I know it so well and can't seem to get rid of even the most trivial things once I'm used to them. They turn into an extension of myself. We're a little our goose-quill pen, we're the table and the inkwell, we're that patch of sunlight, showing the time on the tiles in my humble office-bedroom-parlor-prayer niche. I don't know what drives me to write to you. It's a matter of clearing things up, or if you prefer, joining history to the story of the Bearn family which you knew so well. But I don't know what drives me to attempt this clarification today. For some time now I could have done it, and I don't know why I haven't up to now. Now that Lord Bearn and his Lady Maria-Antònia have been dead for years, I want you to know in what manner a person whose identity will never be known spent a night with the honorable Bearn family's mad and noble scion. And how it ended.

In the attic of a house, which through an inheritance I found myself obliged to alter from top to bottom, there was a trunk. And inside it, at the bottom of everything, under some books with discolored jackets and yellow-streaked pages and among masses of old clothes, I found a letter which told the tale you'll read below. Without wishing to brag, I believe that what it relates will please and amuse you. And I think that, in spite of the time between then and now, it will release you for a while from the melancholy in which the Bearn Palace's overgrown garden left you, with the dahlias and oleander, the rose-bushes which bloom three times a year, the last time very sadly, the cypresses weary from so much stretching, the greens too green and that sun too sunny and the trail left by so many moons, from one end of the island to the other, poisoning water and land and all the salt in the waves of this Mediterranean, basket of sirens, muttering ceaselessly from so much white foam and from the snouts of so many imprisoned fish. I don't wish to tire you further. My name is Eladi Formentí, of the Formentí family, cousins of the Aixes. You'll find the letter enclosed, in which young Bearn, hopelessly attached to his dolls, is spoken of. I copied it because the passage of years – perhaps at one time instead of being in an attic it was in a cellar – has damaged the original and some bits are hard to read. I'll spare you more preambles, cut my commentaries, and here you have the letter, beginning where it should begin:

There are no words to describe young Bearn. He had so much youth, talent, and beauty that all things should have smiled upon him . . . A Greek from the islands with a fancy coat. A seraph. Excess of brain and spirit finished him off in a hurry. Wasted, burned-out, devoured by the fires of the body, which doesn't forgive. Full of life, thirsty for life, he threw himself at the world, and the world doesn't like excesses. When he was small his mother, a noblewoman who was affectedly severe with her son, spoiled him. A lady of caprices, lovely when young, who as soon as she was pregnant dressed herself in pink and lilac and said she wanted a girl. As she was getting into bed, surrounded by lace and linen sheets, each one fresher than the next, she'd say she wanted a girl. As she drank hot chocolate from a china cup, she'd say she wanted a girl. Her husband was getting frantic and told her, caressing her at the same time to calm her down, that they'd take what came, whatever it might be. And she, seductively, would say she wanted a girl like a doll. She gave birth to a son, and it seemed like she didn't even realize it . . . She raised him, and she raised him as if he were that girl she'd wanted, but who had gotten damaged on the way.

Young Bearn's first real toy was a doll as tall as he was. She had dreamy black eyes and a pretty mouth with little rat's teeth that you could see between her lips, which were always slightly open. Her gown had stripes, white and sky-blue, with an embroidered bodice and a little blue ribbon that went in and out. Her hair was black and came down to her waist, parted in the middle, and flowed around her shoulders. The top half was plaited, and the bottom half loose. Between the plaited and the loose, it was tied with a satin ribbon that was an even lighter blue than the stripes on the gown and the little ribbons on the bodice. But it was always different, because the lady lived in a dream-world, making her gowns and more gowns. And at lunch and dinner the doll sat next to young Bearn. And if the boy didn't pay attention she'd encourage him. "Talk with the doll," she'd tell him, "talk to her . . . She may not speak, but she's listening." And it was beautiful to see the boy dressed in hazel-colored velvet, with lace on the ends of his sleeves and around his neck, with heavy curls all around his face and down his back, talking with the doll between spoonfuls and kissing her hand before he got ready for bed. They cut his curls when he got a little older. They separated him from the doll, who remained, with her striped gown, in the china closet inside the curtained chamber that you got to by the secret stairway after crossing the chapel.

More years passed and young Bearn travelled abroad. The only way to become truly cultured, his mother said, who now always dressed in silk during the summer, and in elephant-colored velvet in winter. Young Bearn had teeth like mother-of-pearl, and eyes that glowed like hot coals. After he returned to the island, his teeth lost their brilliance and his eyes that mixture of fire and dark water. He spent hours and hours looking at the doll in the room with the china closet. In the village, they soon started saying that the young master lived shut up in the chamber with the secret staircase, with candles lit until early morning. And they said on some nights you could see his shadow, moving to and fro behind the curtained window, clasping the doll around the neck and picking her up as if she were a real child. He spent two years like this, with the doll. The elder Bearn died. The lady was grief-stricken. She adorned herself with heavy obsidian necklaces, and young Bearn seemed not to be in this world. Till one day he told them to pack his trunks, and he went travelling again. He took short trips and came back tired, with sunken cheeks and flabby skin, bringing lots of dolls. He filled up the china closet room with them. He brought four from Paris, one dressed in Marie-Antoinette's shepherd costume, with a white wig on. From Madrid, a princess of Eboli. From London, an Ophelia and a Portia. He had some Majorcan ones with mittens. And no one knows where he picked up a little box with a doll on the lid,

who when you wound it and the music was going would curt-
sy while she was whirling around. In Rosselló he found some
old ones, unusually well-preserved. And one, the marquise
doll, whose arms and legs and head all moved and who wore a
necklace of pink pearls. By the time he had nearly a hundred, –
some of them, the young ladies, nearly as tall as he was – he
was completely gone. He had beds and cradles brought up to
the room. He brought little tables and scissors and all kinds of
sewing needles and different sized crochet hooks to make the
lace for their petticoats. And precious silks. And thimbles – he
had three dozen, and when he died they found quite a few of
them pierced with little holes, from so much working with the
needle, from so much continuous sewing.

One day his mother, who accepted this madness but didn't
understand it – after accepting it she started to pester him
about it – took advantage of one of his trips to change the lock
on the door to the china closet room, which some time ago had
turned into the dolls' room. And when young Bearn returned,
loaded with little dolls, he found he couldn't set them up. With
the exaggerated sensitivity of those who are mad but have
flashes of clarity, he immediately understood what was going
on and kept quiet. He had the Bearn family's carpenter make a
ladder. And when it was all finished, in front of the gardener
who had so much trouble bending over and straightening up,
and in front of the cook who was telling the gardener he'd have
to increase the parsley patch, he leaned it against the wall and
entered the dolls' room through the window, after breaking a
pane so he could stick his hand through and lift the latch. And
from then on he entered and left through the window, going
up and down the ladder.

On one of those jasmine nights, with an angry moon among
clouds that threaten rain, young Bearn came to see me and said
that since he considered me a good man and knew of my saint-

ly patience, he wanted to show me the dolls. I wish I could tell you the things I saw that night – and more than the things, the kind of presence there was behind the things. Glows that died as soon as you turned your eyes towards them. Beginnings of whispers that stopped suddenly when you tried to listen closely. But I'm afraid I don't know how. On the path, between the blue of the moon and the darker blue of the shadows, I started to feel an uneasiness that had no logical cause. We were walking side by side, without saying a word, and we had to walk for a long time because I lived far away and the Bearns' path was very bad at that time. When we reached the garden, we propped the ladder up against the wall and went in through the window. The first thing he did was light several candles. Since a breeze was coming in from outside, our shadows and the dolls' shadows started dancing on the walls. I didn't have enough eyes to see everything. Dolls standing, lying down, in beds, in cradles, sitting . . . Big dolls with little dolls on their laps. Half-dressed, naked . . . There was a blond one in the very center of the room, her feet nailed to the floor with a nail through the center of each foot. "If I don't nail her down, she falls . . . ," he told me. And when he said it he came up close, with eyes like a sorcerer's, and told me he'd come close so she wouldn't hear, because she didn't know her feet were nailed down. There was another one dressed as a queen, in white damask embroidered with grey pearls from her breast to her waist. Her cape was damask too, lined with silk the color of hot blood, and at the top of the cape, sixteen rows of golden frills. He went up to her and stroked her hair. Then he bent down and kissed the hem of her skirt, and told me I had to kiss it too. He introduced her to me as the most beautiful doll in the world and told me to touch her hand, which was cold like ice.

Then he made me sit down in front of three tall dolls, the young ladies, all of them dressed alike: in soft silk with pale frills on the skirts and ivory silk bows, and bouquets of orange tree flowers mixed in with the frills and a bunch of orange tree flowers in the center of the bodice. He explained to me that these gowns had gotten old and the dolls were fed up with them, because they were rather conceited and were always dying for a change. He showed me a number of colored drawings, which he'd made himself. They showed the young ladies dressed in floating veils, green and pumpkin-colored. He said the green was the leaves and the pumpkin the flowers. They were wearing tiaras topped with rubies as big as cherries. And bracelets. The one in the middle had black ribbons for bracelets, with a bow on each of her wrists. "It's velvet," I heard him say, almost right in my ear. And when he got up – because to show me the drawings he'd sat down beside me – , whether because the madness had started infecting me or because the candle flames flickered a lot in the breeze we made shuffling the papers, the fact is that it seemed like the three dolls were staring at him and the one in the middle, the one who had on the velvet bracelets in the picture, gave a little laugh.

While he was arranging the drawings, young Bearn told me to get the iron ready. He asked me if I had some matches, because he had to make a fire and heat the coals. I told him that though the night might be cool, it wasn't cold enough to make a fire, and he said we'd have to heat the iron, even if we suffocated from it. He sent me over to a small marble table and I saw a clumsy old iron with a little oven inside it and a sock wrapped around the handle. With papers he'd already crumpled up in a basket and some kindling wood, we made a fire in the hearth, and put logs on top of the kindling. We sat on some stools and watched the fire, since he told me it had to be done calmly. And sitting there, we saw a madness of scarlet tongues, whistling and climbing towards the chimney. When everything was ready, he picked up some burning coals in a tiny brass shovel, filled the iron, set it down on the marble table beside some tongs, and said afterwards we'd curl the wigs. Near the tongs and the iron there was a bundle of rags, bound tightly with a blue ribbon. He explained to me that inside was the stub of a candle, and that when the iron was good and hot you could rub it over the flat side and the wax would melt inside the rags and make the metal smooth. But once it had gone over the rags you had to wipe the iron thoroughly, so it wouldn't ruin the clothes that had to be pressed. I remained standing at the foot of the little table, waiting for the iron to get hot. Meanwhile, he was darting around like a weasel. When he passed in front of a big doll he'd give her a quick caress, and he straightened the tilted head of an Amazon, who was sitting on a Moorish horse with crimson trappings. Then he straightened a fold in her skirt. "Naughty thing," he said to her.

A minute later, he took a fancy dress from a sewing box with a mirror inside the lid. He sat down, put his knees together, and set to work sewing. It was a pleasure to see him, with the tip of his tongue between his lips. When he'd sewn everything he wanted to sew, he left the dress on the chair beside him, which I'd sat in to look at the tall dolls, and slowly went over to open the wardrobe in the corner. Half of the right-hand side had shelves up to the top, full of dolls' bald heads. From the center of the left-hand part he took an ironing board, covered with a cotton blanket scorched by irons that had been too hot, and laid it down. Then, with a narrow plank that he got from behind a curtain, he barricaded the door which was never opened, and without even looking at me said, "This'll make it hard for them to get in." He added that whenever he was ironing they'd fiddle with the lock, because they knew he was in the room from the smell of clothes being ironed. And very calmly, he spread the sewn outfit on the ironing board. I didn't know what to think or say. The window, which a moment before had been full of moonlight, was pitch black. It seemed like a long time since we'd climbed the ladder, and I wanted to leave. But I couldn't figure out how to do it. He was so preoccupied with the iron that I started to think he'd fogotten me. But then, suddenly he realized that two of the candles had gone out, and he asked me to go and light them, and while I was up, to trim the ones whose wicks were too long, so they wouldn't flicker. And that I should tread lightly because one of the dolls had been a light sleeper ever since she was little, and if she woke up she'd make a fuss because she was jealous and only wanted him to make gowns for her.

I went on tiptoe to light the two candles, and I trimmed the others. But even though I could hardly be heard, the doll whom he'd told me about when she was little woke up. He said he'd thought I'd wake her, and picked her up very carefully, as if he were afraid she'd break. The striped gown had gotten old, and the satin ribbon on her hair was broken. With the doll in his arms, he went to hunt for the music box. Then he sat down, started it up, put the doll on his knees, and began to rock her as if she were a child with blood in her veins. He smoothed her hair with a trembling hand, and told her that when he was dying she'd still be alive, and no one would think of the dolls, and a very special little girl would have to be born, the kind who when they're little already want to be grown up, and only live to dissolve themselves in some other girl, which would be her, his doll with the striped dress. "Love them," he told her. "You're the most precious of all. Love them." And he took off her shoes. Then he looked at me slightly surprised, as if he didn't know me. After a while, in a very low voice, he asked me if I'd go back to loading the iron, because he needed it very hot to iron some brocade the color of blood pudding. "And afterwards, while you're waiting," he said, "amuse yourself with those little boxes." He kept on rocking the doll, and after filling the iron with coals, I went up to a long table covered with little white boxes with names written on top: pearly vase, crystal tears, slender obsidian and flat obsidian, lake-water emeralds plucked from mountain silt, rhine-stones, sequins – fiery rose, peacock's-eye blue, greens and bright reds, magenta, violet and gold and moon-white.

There was a very small box with an inscription on the lid that said "Can be sewn on backwards." When he realized I was looking at it, he told me it contained the sequins with the most beautiful undersides. And without waiting for me to answer, he got up carefully, as if he were carrying a bouquet of glass or water flowers in his arms, which might break or spill at any moment, and put the doll in the china closet. The iron, mean-while, had gotten so red-hot that we had to leave it on the windowsill for a while. When it was at the temperature he wanted, he asked me if I'd like to iron, because he had to try the sewn dress on a doll from Paris. It gave off a terrible heat. While I was ironing – as best I could, because sometimes the heavy silk would wrinkle under the iron – I watched him out of the corner of my eye, and saw what unspeakable torture he was suffering, trying to put the dress on the doll. He wanted to pull it on over the feet, and one of her legs always stayed out-side it. Finally he got her all dressed, clasped at the waist with a shiny button through a buttonhole. He told me the thing he'd had the most trouble learning was how to make buttonholes, and that in the end he'd learned to make them so well that it seemed like a tailor's work, with a holding loop and every-thing so the buttonhole would come out attractive. What had been especially difficult for him, more than the bit of scallop-ing, was to cut the buttonhole, to cut the cloth, because he was always afraid the cloth would cry and blood would come out. He asked me if I knew how to embroider, and whether I'd like to help with it. He wanted to embroider each doll's name on her gowns, so he wouldn't put one doll's clothes on another. Sometimes he made mistakes, and then they got excited and kicked up a fuss, for they only wanted to wear things that were theirs. I told him I didn't know how to embroider, but I knew an embroideress who also made lace. He clapped his hand over my mouth with such force and fury that I was really worried until he took it off. His eyes were popping out of his head and he was breathing unpleasantly. "You're a simpleton," he muttered, "a simpleton, but you don't know what you're saying . . ." He quickly calmed down, and told me he didn't want to have anything to do with ladies.

And without further explanation, he blew out all the candles, and we were plunged into darkness, with just that bit of scarlet brightness from the ash-covered coals that remained in the fireplace. I turned my head. Everything was black night. After a moment, the moonlight came through the window as if it were coming from another world, lighting up the gowns on the dolls. The little sequins sparkled, and the dark jewels and the folds in the satin. He was quiet, and it was like he'd fallen asleep. In a voice that seemed barely human, he told me the dolls weren't evil. Yes, perhaps there were some who got annoyed easily, but it didn't last long. "What harm can they do, with pasteboard and porcelain heads, bones made of perforated iron, wooden legs and bellies full of sawdust . . . ?" And he choked on his words. "What harm can they do . . . ?" Not knowing how to console him, I put my hand on his shoulder and in a very low voice said "Let's go." "Yes," he answered, "let's go. Tomorrow I'll have to work hard." But when we were going to climb out the window, we found they'd taken away the ladder. He grabbed my arm, and with his face next to mine said "My mother's punishing me . . . she smelled the iron and wants me to spend the night with the dolls." And he went over to the one who was closest to him and said "Look how the moonbeam rests on her shoulders." But I went to the door, took away the plank, and while I was looking at the lock to see if I could pry it off I heard him say "Don't do it."

We spent the night in the dolls' room. A night which never ended. Before I fell asleep my legs fell asleep. When I moved them it was like they were inside an anthill. From time to time I was awakened by some kind of uneasiness, which I'm sure didn't come from that bit of death which climbed up to my knees with thousands of feverish little legs . . . I don't know if I dreamt it, but I still remember some barely visible shadows, which changed position without me ever being able to see them move. And unexpected sounds: smothered moans as if the dolls, furious at not being left alone, were coming towards me with their mouths full of curses, biting their tongues to hold them in. Hurried scamperings along the wall, on tiptoe . . . a cock's cry, strangled in midair, a cock who seemed to be in a corner of the room under three layers of blankets . . . And above all, a thick hum, with highs and lows, that made me think maybe I'd fallen asleep on top of a swarm of bees – all held down with great effort, about to explode. At dawn the ladder was put up beneath the window. We silently climbed down into the garden, which was full of half-open white roses, with the buds' first leaves all curled, rusty and poisonous-looking around the edges. The half-opened roses must have gotten dusty, and the rain, instead of washing them, had blackened them. And I felt strange, as if something had snapped inside me.

A week later, one of the Bearns' servants came looking for me at daybreak. They'd found the young master lying underneath the window, his face down and the ladder on top of him. I dashed off in a panic. He was really dead, surrounded by servants. They told me the lady had fainted and they were reviving her, making her drink brandy with lemon juice. I asked for help, and turned him over with his face up, after taking the ladder off him. His eyes were open, glassy like a doll's. And the tongs thrust into his belly. I don't know why, we went up, we crossed the chapel, climbed the secret staircase, and broke down the door to the room. There were lots of dolls splattered with blood, and the one from the china closet was on the floor with her legs torn out. Against the window, leaning unsteadily, was the doll with the pierced feet. The nails were still there, half pulled out. In the tops of her feet, you could see the round holes from where they'd been hammered in. A gust of air made her fall on her back, facing the ceiling. Her eyes were glassy like young master Bearn's.

They closed the room forever. When I think of it sometimes, I see the dolls, grown dusty now, with their hair dishevelled and linked by many, many spiderwebs ... their faces and clothes discolored by time's peace, which is the peace I crave for myself, and which I crave in eternity for whoever reads these lines. To whoever may read them, goodbye and amen.

A Flock of Lambs in All Colors

WHEN SOMEONE asks me if I like children, you could defi-
nitely say he's sticking his finger where he shouldn't stick it . . .
No, no, I don't like them. They drive me crazy! I spend hours
and hours in the park. One day I sat down beside a very pretty
nursemaid and the gardener, who I think was pruning a rosebush, since I can't distinguish plants or trees or flowers either –
from time to time he looked at me and winked, as if to say
"What luck!" He hadn't noticed that I only had eyes for the
child, who was making a pile of sand. With her little fingers
she'd grab the ants trying to crawl up the hill and throw them
away.

The nursemaid . . . What interest can I have in a nursemaid?
What I'd like is a tableful of boys and girls. Mine . . . The girl
who was throwing the ants away wore a dress with a puff of
lace on it. She had blond ringlets, halfway down her back. So
tiny . . . And I always carry marbles in my pocket, in case I see a
child who pleases me . . . that is, if it doesn't seem like I'm
scaring them. I've never given any away. I don't dare to. I'm

about to stick my hand in my pocket and get one when my hand starts shaking, and I give it up. The doctor told me it was my father's fault. A tableful of children . . . and a butler standing beside it, so that if I forget one of their names he can whisper it in my ear. And the butler and the children, all of them, would laugh to see me so absent-minded. Because I couldn't remember all their names, and Neus I'd called Maria-Antònia, and Pere I'd called Enric . . .

What use has money been to me in my life? How often I've asked myself that question! I fell in love with a girl I met at a costume ball, dressed as a shepherdess. She was like an angel. A real angel. "You're too much in love," said the doctor I had at that time. But he didn't understand it. The one who figured it out was the man who told me I was going around with a wounded psyche. He made me talk and talk. And one day, when he'd learned all my secrets, he took off his glasses, and wiping the lenses with a little piece of cloth, told me it was all my father's fault. But he didn't cure me, and when I leave a park I always have tears in my eyes. When I'm there I can't do anything, it's like a sickness . . .

In my home, the old house in the village, we had an enclosed gallery on the second floor. Three doors led into it: one from my bedroom, one from my parents' bedroom, and one from the sitting room between them. There were some elegant chairs in the sitting room, upholstered with cream-colored velvet, with the backs and legs gilded. In the middle of the gallery was a wicker table, surrounded by four armchairs that made a set with it. And two rocking chairs, one in each corner, with lace doilies where you put your head, tied with shiny pink silk ribbons. I can see it as if I were still there. One afternoon, my father punished me because they'd put donkey's ears on me at school. "Get up there," he said, "and don't let me see you again!" I sat down in a rocking chair and started rocking. I was looking at the colored windowpanes in the gallery. There were white ones and blue ones that made a column, alternating from top to bottom. At the top, stretching from one side to the other, there was a frieze of yellow panes. Down at the bottom, a frieze of lavender panes. And between the two friezes and the ones that formed the column there were green and red and plum-colored panes. Anything you can imagine! The plum-colored ones were iris petals, with green glass leaves on the stalks. The gallery looked out on the field, and the field went towards the mountain, divided by a path with wheel ruts. And from rocking so much and so much looking at all those colors, lit up by the setting sun so they stained the gallery's walls and floor, I got dizzy. To overcome my dizziness, I stood up and stuck my nose against a red pane.

At that moment the flock came down. You could hear bells ringing and the dog was barking. Then the first lamb came in sight. All red. Then came more, and as they came down I started running from one pane to another in order to see them. And now there was a plum-colored lamb behind an iris petal, and next to him a blue one, and a green one in midair . . . I crouched down as far as I could go, since the lavender panes were at the bottom, and I saw three lavender lambs . . . And when I wanted to see them yellow – the yellow panes made the frieze all the way at the top – the flock had already passed. I went back to sitting in the rocking chair, quiet as a mouse and happy as a nightingale, I mean a lark, since they say all nightingales are sad . . . Happy as a lark, but with all the joy inside me. And my father came looking for me, to make me come down to dinner. I ate the whole time with my eyes lowered, and my father looked at me darkly because he must have thought I was miserable from the punishment. The next day, after coming home from school, I kissed his hand and snuck back up to the gallery. The flock took forever to come, and when I heard the dog barking I grabbed the table and pulled it over to the window, and put an armchair on top of the table, and with a great deal of difficulty, a golden chair on top of the armchair. And when the first lamb came in sight I watched it through a blue pane, and then through an iris, and then through the green leaves, and the lambs kept passing and I kept looking at them changing color, from one side to the other, and there were red ones that weren't the same shade of red, some lighter and some darker, and finally I climbed all the way up and the last few lambs were all yellow ... This delirium lasted for days. Then one afternoon, when I was up there with my feet on the cream-colored velvet, so delicate, of the golden chair, I heard a great shout behind me: "You're too old now to act like a jackass!" It was my father. I jumped with fright, the chair slipped, and everything came tumbling down: the chair, the armchair, and me from on top of the chair. I broke one of my arms, near the elbow, and the doctor said I was very lucky, that it could have killed me.

When I got married I was very much in love. I'd just taken my exams, not because I needed them to live, but because at that time I thought making four bits of Latin comprehensible to two dozen unfortunates was something very worthwhile ... So I got married, madly in love, and on our wedding night, when I saw that angel of God beside me, I felt a great joy like when I saw the lambs in all those colors. What they call the joy of life ... but stronger ... mixed with a kind of taste of childhood ... *Et ecce infantia mea olim mortua est et ego vivo* ... There are no words to convey the feeling. But all at once, like a stone hitting my forehead, I heard my father's shout and it seemed like I was falling and I was struck half-dead. A great misfortune. My wife was very young and innocent, and I didn't know how to tell her what I was going through ... After some years she asked for a separation because she hated me. And no one will ever know how much I loved her . . . She was my wife, and the child I couldn't have, and I treated her as if she were a three-year-old girl. Come, little one, what would you like me to buy you? I wanted to buy her dolls. I stopped at all the store windows and thought: I'll buy her this little black and white horse with the red patent leather bridle, and those arrows with green and black feathers at the ends, and this little theater with a curtain that rises and falls, and this little dog with his tail lopped off who can walk. When the three magi came I went crazy . . . when I saw so many children lining up to put letters in the magus' cardboard mailbox, asking for balls and marbles and guns.

I had a mistress. I really don't know why. Perhaps because I needed to be with someone, and because it still gave me a few hopes. She was an artiste, an indescribable girl, heaven and hell all mixed up together. She sang . . . The things I had to hear! And loaded with money and health. To give away and to sell. I, who would have liked not one child or two, but a table-ful. And to hear their shouts and laughter. By now they'd be all grown up, and it'd be time for a new wave of children – grand-children, all mine. In the summertime, when I go to the vil-lage, I'm fascinated by the brood hen. Roosting, all puffed up, with the chicks coming out from under her and from under her wings. And towards evening I sit in the rocking chair in the gallery, the same one as before, only a little changed. As I gaze at the colored panes, I doze off slightly and lean back in the chair. In my grogginess it seems like there are children hang-ing on my legs and clambering up over my chest. And I lean as far back as I can, so they won't have trouble climbing. And they touch my face with their soft little hands . . . Just like a mother cat and her kittens. All around and on her back . . . hot and small.

Love

I HATE to make you open up when you've just closed, but your sewing shop's the only one I pass when I get off work. I've been looking in your window for a while now. It's silly, a guy my age, filthy with cement and worn out from running along the scaffold . . . Let me wipe the sweat off my neck. The cement dust gets in the wrinkles in my skin, and it burns when it mixes with the sweat. I'd like to . . . you've got everything in the window except what I'd like . . . but maybe that's because it's not nice to put it in the window. You've got string, needles, all kinds of thread. I can see how this thread thing must drive women half-crazy . . . When I was little I used to empty my mother's sewing basket. I'd put the spools on a knitting needle and have a good time spinning them around. It makes you laugh that something like that'd be fun for a lug like me. But you know, that's how life is. Today's my wife's Saint's Day, and I'm sure by now she thinks I won't give her a thing, that I forgot all about it. The sewing shop ladies, sometimes they've got what I want inside those big cardboard boxes . . . How about a necklace? But she doesn't like them. When we got married I gave her a glass one with sherry-colored beads, and I asked her if she liked it and she said "Yes, very much." And she never wore it even once. And when I'd ask her, just once in a while so it wouldn't get on her nerves, "Why don't you wear the necklace?," she'd say it was too dressy, and how when she put it on she felt like a china cabinet. And I couldn't change her mind. Rafelet, our first grandson, who was born with tons of hair and six toes on each foot, used the beads for marbles. I guess you think it's funny, but some things are hard for a man. Send me out to buy any kind of food. I'm not the type who gets embarrassed carrying a shopping basket. On the contrary, I enjoy choosing meat. I've been pals with the butcher ever since we were born. Or choosing fish. The fish lady – her folks, that is – used to sell fish to mine. But to buy anything besides food . . . I'm dizzy as an owl in daylight . . . Give me some advice. What do you think I should get her . . . two dozen spools of thread? . . . different colors, but especially black and white since they're colors you always need? Maybe that's what she'd like best. But who knows? Maybe she'll throw them at my head. It depends what kind of mood she's in. If she's in a bad mood, she treats me like a child . . . After thirty years of marriage, a man and a woman . . . It all comes from too much trust. That's what I always say. So much sleeping together, so many deaths and births and so much daily bread . . . Or some ribbons? No, that's no good. A lace collar? Yes, maybe a lace collar. She had one all covered with roses, with buds and leaves. The only thing missing was the thorns, I'd tell her as a joke every time she was sewing it on a dress. But she doesn't get dressed up anymore. Her whole life is the house. She's a housewife. If you could see how she makes everything shine . . . the glasses in the dining room cabinet, God Almighty, she must wipe them three times a day with a dustcloth. She picks them up, just barely touching them, puts them on top of the table, and twists the cloth around inside. And then puts them back in order, all in a row, like soldiers with big hats. And the bottoms of the pots! . . . it's like she cooked the food somewhere else instead of inside them. Everything in the house smells clean. What do you think I do when I get home – pick up the paper or listen to the radio? . . . I find a tub full of water on the porch, already warmed by the sun. She makes me soap myself and rinses me off with a watering can. We have a special curtain, with green and white stripes, so the neighbors can't see me. And in winter, she has me wash in the kitchen. What a job it is for her afterwards, mopping up all the water I spill on the floor. And if my hair's too long she scolds me a little. And every week she cuts my nails . . . Well, as far as the lace collar goes, I'm not sure . . . Or some hanks of wool so she can make herself a sweater? But I don't know which ones she'd need . . . And to buy wool in this hot weather and give her something that'd make more work for her . . . Let me read what it says is inside the boxes. Gold buttons, silver buttons, bone buttons, dull buttons. Pin cushions. Boys' undershirts. Dress socks. Patterns. Combs. Shawls. I guess I better decide soon, cause if I don't you'll end up pushing me out the door. Now that we've talked, and I feel like I can trust you, you know what I'd really like? Some panties, long ones with frilly lace on the bottom, and a ribbon that winds in and out the holes in the lace, with the two ends tied in a fancy bow. Have you got any? . . . It was so hard for me to tell you. She'll be crazy with joy. I'll lay them out secretly on the bed, and she'll get a big surprise. I'll tell her: go change the sheets. She'll go change them and find the panties. Oh! The top's gotten stuck. These big boxes are hard to open and close. There we go. So much trouble over nothing. This is the kind I like, with the frilliest lace, so it's just like foam at the bottom . . . Blue ribbon? No. Pink is a happier

color. They won't tear right away, will they? . . . She works so
hard, and never takes even a minute's break . . . At least
choose some that are reinforced. They seem strong to me, and
if you say so too . . . And it's made of cotton? Very strongly
sewn. She'll notice that right away. But she won't say a word
about it. "I like them," she'll say. And that's it. She's a woman
of few words, but she always says what's on her mind. What
size? Now I'm really lost. Let's see, lay them out . . . You know
her? She's round as a little pumpkin. With her thighs, she'll
need the largest waist you've got. They look like dolls' clothes.
When she was twenty they'd have fit her perfectly . . . but
we're older now. Of course you can't do anything about it.
Neither can I. The thing is, I don't see anything else she might
like. She always wants something practical. What'll I do now?
I certainly can't show up empty-handed. Maybe I'll buy something at the pastry shop on the corner . . . No, that's no good. A
working man has so little time for the finer things . . .

The Elephant

WHY DON'T YOU come a little closer? Get under my umbrella . . . I've seen you before, walking up and down in front of the serpent-eaters' cage. The serpent-eater's one kind of bird I don't care for. Some animals do really strange things. Of course, I realize that to throw a snake up in the air over and over again and trample it to death isn't abnormal in a bird that lives on snakes. But I prefer the chameleon. One flick of his tongue and it's *ora pro nobis* . . . This drizzle fills my heart with peace. Yesterday, before getting into bed, I stuck my head out the window. There was a little cloud in the west, and I thought we'd have rain today, and just look at it! I like it, don't think I don't. Especially since it's Sunday. The grey light makes you want to stay in bed, with the leaves all hanging down and the umbrellas, that supremely clever artifact. If it weren't for the spokes it'd be perfect. Weren't you ever scared someone'd stick an umbrella spoke in your eye? Maybe it's something that never happened in your whole life, but you can't reason with fear. Don't you think so? I always think I've got it pointed just

right and that if the umbrella sways just a little and the spoke
gets in your eye it's all . . .

Look, look, he's coming out! When I see him come out of his
house, and walk towards us so very calmly . . . See how he's
raising his trunk? He's just been sleeping, and he's still got
straw on his back. He breathes the rain-fresh air, and salutes
us as he passes . . . You know who established the order of the
elephant? Canute IV, a twelfth-century Danish king. You see?
He probably doesn't know you nearly as well as me, so he's
watching you out of the corner of his eye. That is, he's studying you. If you weren't sitting beside me, he'd be up against
the bars by now with his trunk stretched out, begging for
crackers . . . That's it, Canute IV, of Denmark. Doesn't that
seem strange? Christian V reorganized it, in the year sixteen
ninety-three. I know it by heart. And it says it was modified in
the year . . . wait . . . I have it filed away in my head. What
happens is that sometimes there are files I have to pull and pull
before I can get them open . . . the year eighteen hundred and
eight. My most highly developed memory is for dates. Eighteen hundred and eight. Who knows where we were . . . Isn't it
nice sitting here, listening to the rain beating against the
stretched cloth? Almost no one comes here on rainy days.
They hole up when it's raining. Especially Sunday mornings.
Isn't it nice to breathe this scent of fresh leaves and clean earth,
with this fine big animal here in front of us? You must think
everything connected with elephants interests me. You see?
The medal shows an elephant holding up a tower, and the
tower's held in place by a blue ribbon that goes under the elephant's belly, from one side to the other. Pretty, isn't it? Those
who the king admitted to the order wore white satin hose and
red velvet coats with tails, and feathered hats. They were very
well dressed, don't you think?

Sh, sh . . . Make him think you're not looking, so you won't frighten him ... But notice how he's coming closer ... If we talk like nothing's happening, soon he'll stick his trunk over the railing ... Shu-Yu-Hua, a Siamese king, founded the order of the elephant in the year eighteen ninety. A medal with a red ribbon, edged with green. The colors are separated by two bands, one blue and one yellow ... Now he's got his back to us ... Want to see how I make him turn his head in a jiffy? The minute he hears me crumpling the paper bag. Look how he's wiggling his ears and pretending not to notice. The shameless creature! This weather must be getting on his nerves. Neither sun nor rain, just this bit of pitter-patter. He never does this on sunny days ... he sticks his trunk over the bars like a man as soon as he hears the paper crumpling ... let's try something else. Here mousie, don't you want a little crackie? I call him mousie because he's the same color as a rat. I don't know how the hell he got such wrinkly skin. Hold the umbrella, if you don't mind. Here little one, here. He's never acted indifferent like this. Maybe it's because he doesn't like you. Or maybe he's sick. In the afternoon the zoo fills up with children who stuff him with pieces of bread. He eats them to be polite. But by now he's sick of it, always bending his head with his trunk between his tusks. It's a question of patience.

While he's on his high horse, I'll read you what Fabra's dictionary says. I've got it copied out on this piece of paper I always carry in my wallet. He starts with "Elephant," and then puts masculine gender. He says it's a mammal of the proboscidian group, the largest of all terrestrial animals, with thick skin ... *that* we already knew ... hairless, with an elongated nose in the form of a prehensile trunk ... don't you like that word ... prehensile ... and two very long incisors, eyeteeth, which furnish the bulk of all commercial ivory. Those little arching figures! ... There are two species: the Indian elephant and the African elephant ... In India they paint them. Did you ever see it in newsreels? They paint red leaves with a gold border, and green and blue, and bring them along to their festivals. The force of an elephant is terrifying. They can level a forest with blows of their trunks. Finally . . . he still hasn't moved? Now I understand; the umbrella scares him. Let's close it. It's raining so lightly, it's not worth the trouble of keeping it open. And now let's be quiet for a while and watch. What did I tell you? Look how all of a sudden he's making his trunk dance and laughing because we understood him . . . Look, look how he's lifting his trunk above his head. Mousie! Quick, hold the bag for me. Here, good lad . . . Did you see how politely he took the cracker and put it in his mouth? I've always said we have nothing to teach the animals. It's they who . . . Come on boy, another cracker. Come on now Mr. Elephant, as Mariona used to say, eat your breakfast. She was my little girl. The stork brought her when we were already old, and my wife didn't . . . Every Sunday we'd come see the elephant . . . Look, look how he's stuffing himself. I go without sugar in my coffee so I can bring him crackers.

And wait, you still haven't seen everything. When he hears me crumple up the bag and sees me throw it in the trash basket – which means the cracker-eating game is over – he gets down on his knees and bows to me. Let me have the bag. Now you'll see. See? I'm the one who taught him that. I make him work a little. If you could have seen how Mariona laughed, with the elephant. The day I explained to her all about those gentlemen with satin hose and red coats and the elephant with the tower on his back we were sitting like you and I are sitting now . . . And was she ever wide-eyed! She was quiet all the way home. You could see she was thinking about what I'd said, and she grabbed my hand and squeezed it hard . . . She became more mischievous the year before she died . . . she'd take my shoehorn, which I always keep in the night-table drawer, and put it in my overcoat pocket. I have no idea how she did it because I never saw her. I never said a word. Every time I found the shoehorn in my pocket, I'd put it back in the night-table drawer without saying anything . . . The poor darling! Sometimes I think I didn't love her enough. Even then my friends would tell me: a man's no good for bringing up a girl. After she died, I read someplace that grownups don't understand children, because they're still part of the heaven we put inside them when we make them, which we no longer remember . . . Maybe she would have liked it if I'd said "The shoehorn again?," pretending I was angry to make her laugh. But I thought it was okay not to say anything, that we'd make a game out of that . . .

The first day I had her give a cracker to the elephant – if you'll excuse my saying so – she was shitting in her pants. But when she saw the little mouse take the cracker like he did just now, with that fleshy tweezer, so elegantly . . . she laughed and jumped up and down. She was my queen. Look, there's only one cracker left . . . And I thought he was sick. These crackers must be much less to him than a lump of sugar, don't you think? You can fit a lot of food inside an elephant. Go on boy, here's the last one! And now comes the good part. Watch closely, you see? I crumple up the bag, very slowly, I stretch out my arm calmly, with great calm . . . look how his gaze follows my arm . . . and bam! I throw away the bag. And now we have the bow. Such delicacy! I don't know if you've noticed how the figurines made from elephant tusks have a kind of grace . . . And now I'll be off home to make my dinner. I see it's starting to clear up, and if the sun comes out, this place'll be jammed in no time. Let's go. If you want to go to the serpent-eaters' cage, I'll walk with you a little. It's on my way.

The River and the Boat

"IF YOU LIKE rowing, behind the woods there's the river and the boat," my friend's wife said. They'd invited me to spend the weekend on their estate, and everyone knew how I liked water. I remember my mother saying, in a kind of anxious rush, that when I was very young I'd laugh when they bathed me. And when they wrung the sponge out over me, I'd open my mouth like a fish. I had my first intense experience of rain in the country house where we spent the summers. One night it rained continuously. I got up to look at the water. The darkness frightened me, but I went out on the terrace and lay down on the stones. The rain fell in my mouth. I drank and my fear went away. I thought of how that water was the water which filled the fountains. And every day I'd stir the fountain with a reed, so the water would dry up quickly, and ask the clouds for more rain.

I learned how to swim in the river. There was a sandy island in the middle, a small one. I'd stretch out with my legs in the water, close my eyes, and pretend I was going around the world, carried along by the current. My thirst is indescribable. A wild craving for the taste, the freshness of water on my gums. A passion to feel the water go down my throat. A glass of water, my hand in the water, my cheek beneath the water, my bath ... I don't like salt water. My water's fresh water, springtime water. Water with reeds, with the shadows of leaves on the banks. Shallow water, transparent, with pebbles on the bottom. Flowing water. Salt water attacks, fresh water carries you away. Fresh water dreams never end.

I got up at daybreak. It was windy, and some dried-up leaves blew around me, fallen too soon. My friends must have still been asleep. Seen from the outside, the house looked strangely deserted, as if no one had ever lived there. The woods sloped down towards the river, but the river couldn't be seen because the tall grass blocked it off, along with a row of ancient willows. A bird called; a magpie in the sky above the treetops. Another followed it, with blue-black feathers and wingtips white as salt. I went through the woods, still grey from the dawn, when the herbs' heady smells start mingling. The water glistened, speckled with light and shadow. The first ray of sunlight that filtered through the branches died upon the water and was reborn in the depths, hesitant, a white web. The rushes grew straighter when the row of willows ended. The bank was covered with grass. Behind a bush like a frozen fire, dotted with flame-colored balls, I found the boat. Green, with the paint chipped and dry. The oars were black, as if they'd been smeared with tar. Among the reeds, against the keel of the boat, a doll was rocking to and fro, her head split open. The bottom of her dress, rotten with time and water, was ringed by little leaves.

I went for a swim before getting in the boat. The water was dense. Not fresh; stagnant. The river seemed more like a narrow lake than a real river, so green I could hardly see my arms when the water covered them. I swam awhile. Afterwards, sitting in the boat, I looked at my hands. I'd spent ten minutes in the water, but the skin around my nails was white and wrinkled as if I'd been in all morning. When I was about to pick up the oars, I got the urge to rest a little. With my eyes shut and my head raised, the breeze and the insects' gentle buzzing – a moment before, there'd been a bee like a drop of gold on the edge of the boat – made me half-sense the way in which all things slowly revolve, the land and the water, this island of grain and rocks and trees, held in place by waves of light and night. And I started rowing with the black oars. The boat was clumsy. The river was like oil, and the oars grew heavier with each stroke. Leaving a clump of reeds behind, I passed beneath a leafy arch. Up above, the wind set the green leaves blazing and then darkened them. But instead of making me joyous, that struggle of transparencies in the shadow's mouth pricked at my heart a little, as if something were saying good-bye. Suddenly, the brightest greens died. The wind had stopped, and now only the dead leaves on top of the water moved – a roof of rusty colors that ripped with each stroke of the oars. The air rising from the water made me drowsy. Further on, there'd surely be bright-cheeked flowers, and the sun would pour down on everything, but the light on the water was dark and weary. I saw how the river was narrowing, and the trunks were thicker, all covered with moss, aglow with that hot wetness which stuck to my skin.

Quite some time passed and, without realizing it, I stopped rowing. You couldn't hear a thing. Not even the scurrying of some little animal, or a birdcall. Something was starting to change inside me, and a strange fever blurred my senses. I started rowing again. The boat moved forward more slowly than ever, even though I was rowing with great force. Half-instinctively, I glanced at one of the oars just as I was lifting it out of the water. It seemed to have gotten shorter. Barely half the other one remained, and it was bending like a young branch. Something in the depths was eating the wood, taking it from me without the slightest effort. "If you like rowing . . ."—I heard my friend's wife's voice. But I couldn't remember anything about her, and I'd almost have sworn that I'd never known her. You couldn't see so much as a finger of earth or a spot of sunlight. Everything was green and black. The river was narrowing, and soon the boat would just barely be able to scrape between the banks. By this time the oars were useless. If I'd wanted to go back, I'd have had to get out of the boat and leave it there, and my friends would have asked me what I'd done with it, and I'd have had to explain that the river had narrowed and the trees had made a wall . . .

A white feather fell, and lay flat on the water, which hadn't even reflected it. The trees were no longer trees and the leaves were no longer leaves. I could only remember that doll with her head split open. A long time had passed . . . and my breath was short and difficult. I felt like my eyes were swelling and I couldn't shut them. I touched them, and they were round. In the landscape, all shadows, an expectation throbbed like the instant before a childbirth. I still tried to row, from pure instinct, and the oarless boat moved forward slightly. But I was suffocating, and it was my suffocation that pushed me forward. I opened my mouth as wide as I could to let in a stream of air, but the air had gotten thick and it ripped at the sides of my mouth. And when I could no longer breathe at all and felt like my whole body was tied in knots, I started shaking and kicking holes with my feet in the boat, which seemed to have turned to mud. I felt a terrible pressure on both sides of my neck, and the boat was melting beneath me, and I was alone with the death that was welling up inside me, quickly, like a poisonous weed. A kind of dizziness threw me forward and I fell flat on the water like that white feather, with my legs stuck fast to the surface. Some bony fins had grown from both sides of my chest, and in the middle, a scaly pectoral. I tried to swim with my arms, but I couldn't even remember where they were. And then I felt a huge membranous fin, rising painfully all the way down my back. And a gentle whirlpool was sucking me down in the water. Innocent, I started to swim. Everything was fresh and easy. Divine. I'd become a fish. And I stayed one for many years.

The Gentleman and the Moon

HE TOLD ME not to be startled at seeing his face so white. "If my face is white it's because . . ." And he put his hand over his mouth and rolled his eyes, as if a huge shudder was going through him. He was an old man, very tall, thin with boatlike feet. Sunken cheeks, with small deep-set eyes. Delicate lips, very strange, like the lips on a young woman's mouth. The skin on his face was strikingly white, motionless. A little white face marked by an occasional cavity. "Yes," he said, "my body and face are white. My whole skin. Pocked and scorched. But before, some five years ago, I was nothing like this. Everything started when I sold my shop and bought a little house. I retired because I was worn out. I didn't need much. I could live on what I had. I'd gotten tired of my shop. But all of a sudden, now that I didn't have it, I started to miss it sometimes, and I felt a little out-of-place in the middle of everything. A man who's alone develops manias after a while . . . little manias . . . manias you can't tell anyone about, because someone else's manias almost always make you laugh. Manias which help keep you going, which help you make it through the day to the night and the night to the day, from one month to another and one year to the next . . . manias which keep you company."

He looked at me very seriously for a while, not saying anything, and finally, just when I'd started to think he'd told me everything, he continued: "Whether it was hot or cold, clear or cloudy, I'd go out for a stroll in the garden, all dressed-up, when night came. Yes, I'd gotten in the habit of strolling around the garden every night, all dressed-up. I'd spend the day cleaning and straightening up the house, because even more than a man who lives by himself, I'm a solitary man. No one entered my house. I did everything myself. I sewed on buttons, mended clothes when they needed it, brushed my suits and ironed my pants. I shined my own shoes. There wasn't a man in the world as neat as I was. The hardest thing for me was folding the sheets, but I managed that too. To stroll through my garden, dressed in pinstriped pants, fancy boots, bowler hat, and a fine handkerchief in my breast pocket, made me feel just great. I'd take my walking stick when the sky was clear, and my umbrella when it was raining . . . I'd go out like I was on my way to a party, stroll around a bit, day-dreaming, and think how I was going to organize my work the next day. My garden was pretty. Old walls with caked plaster, ivy and rosebushes here and there, and pieces of glass stuck on top of everything. Pieces of glass from green and white bottles, and occasionally one that was brown, the color of burnt caramel. In the middle of the garden stood a big circular fountain. I always kept it empty, because it'd broken as soon as I moved in, and stagnant water attracts mosquitos. And in the wall at the far end, among the climbing plants, was a little door that opened onto the fields.

"One night I found it open. It had opened all by itself, or else I'd left it open when I went to take out the garbage . . . I don't

know which. But it was open, and the strangest part was that
through the opening in the door came a very bright ray of
moonlight, which stopped just in front of the fountain. The
whole garden without moonlight. Only that ray, which had
snuck in like a thief. I started walking along it very calmly, like
a great lord. I stuck my head through the doorway, and I saw
how it went straight up to the moon. That's all I saw and,
walking and walking, . . . I don't care whether you believe me
or not . . . of course I'd prefer if you did believe me, because
blessed are those who believe . . . but if you don't want to believe me . . . Believe it or not, I found myself on the moon. I
can't tell you how it happened, because when you're very surprised you don't stop and think. I know I went for a walk, and
this great uneasiness welled up inside me. And then, all at
once, I turned tail and rushed back down the moonbeam.
When I got to the bottom I went in through the little door and
bolted it shut. I went straight into the house. I slept; twelve
straight hours, just like a newborn child. And the next day it
was the same. The door open, the moonbeam like a path lit up
by angels, and me on top of it. Very calm. And carrying an
umbrella, because while I was getting dressed I'd glanced out
the window and it looked a little cloudy . . .

"And what happened on the moon? I've been expecting that
question for a while. Well then. On the moon, nothing the first
few days. Lots of light, that's for sure, because the moonlight
on earth is very different from the moonlight on the moon. On
the earth the moonlight's spread out, while on the moon it's all
packed together. The night's huge paws hold it down, and we
only see what escapes from between the fingers . . . The
ground was silk, the color of white petals. During the first few
days, my emotions kept me from seeing anything. It took me
quite a while to realize certain things, because at that moment,
and from far away, everything looked the same: the flour

mountains and snow mountains they have there, the mead-
ows of leafless gardenias, and the big ponds full of milk with
sleeping swans. The clean sheets scattered about ... What
happened to me can only be compared ... I'm sorry, I can't
even find a comparison. And that secret ... the secret which
made me laugh while I was sweeping the dining room floor, or
washing the only dish that got dirty ... which gave me the
urge to laugh when some poor jerk walked by – someone like
you, who didn't know where the mills are that you can't see by
day or night, the transparent cows, drunk on anisette and water, the strange descending intrigues of the jasmines, magno-
lias, and tuberoses, the whitewashers' graveyard ... I thought
if they could only see me, all dressed-up at night, going out
through the little door on my way to the moon. And not once
or twice, but every night, every blessed moonlit night, every,
every, every, every night ... And while I was doing house-
work and hanging out shirts on the terrace, I'd be saying in a
soft voice, like a song: every, every, every night ...

"One afternoon, when I was sweeping up some leaves that
fall had blown onto my sand, I saw something shining that
wasn't a bit larger than a lentil. White and almost like glass. I
put it in my pocket and thought, just for a moment, like a flash,
that maybe it was a bead from a necklace that had gotten mixed
in with the sand before they'd strung it. But that night, on the
moon, I found more of them. It must have been the weather,
because at first I hadn't seen any ... Some of those lentils had
buds, very delicate buds, like the thinnest kind of thread, size
sixty or seventy, strands which seemed fragile, but which absolutely couldn't be broken. And the next day I found lots
more of them, all around the fountain in a big circle. They must
have fallen from the moon when I was there, and then taken
root all by themselves and budded and grown like things pos-
sessed, with a plant fury that made you shudder. I chewed on

one. I had to spit it out; it was bitter like clover. And those above, the ones that budded on the moon, sent their shoots downwards, as if they were seeking the ones around the fountain. And soon afterwards, a shaft started coming down and another one rising. But the day I decided to climb up it, they were still a long way from meeting. And I got in the habit of not going to the moon on the beam that came through the doorway, but through my shaft. When I came to the end of it, I'd cross over to the other part on the pathway made by the light. And during the day those threads couldn't be seen, because they were lost in the sunlight.

"One evening, I decided I wouldn't get dressed-up anymore to go to the moon. No sir, I had work to do! . . . And I went out in shirtsleeves and corduroy pants, carrying some pruning shears and a bunch of short ropes for tying together the strands that were out of place. And I joined the ones above to the ones below, so the shaft would be strong, smooth, and round, with all the strands in order. I spent my nights working with great gusto, up and down. Now I plait them because there's an empty space, now I fasten them to make it safer, now I cut them off because there's too much . . . I slept all day, and as soon as it was dark the big job began . . . up we go, up we go . . . from one side to the other, pull over here where it seems crooked, smooth it down up higher where it's wrinkled, worry about this piece because it's too thin, look, watch, touch and listen, twine and untwine, make four knots because it seems like everything's going to fall . . . to make sure it won't tear, tighten the weft so no light can get in . . . keep on the move . . . run up higher where it seems to bulge. A cut with the scissors, a sliding knot, stop up that hole as best you can, patch up that tear with spit, throw open your arms when you come to a narrow part . . . And the day I had the shaft finished and perfect, like interwoven silk threads, I rested. I lay down inside the fountain, with my hands folded behind my head. And I started laughing with the night, almost without realizing it, with the moon shining right down on top of me. And every night I'd enjoy the moon for a while. At first dressed, but then later on totally naked. I'd work a little, I'd straighten the strands that a flight of birds had messed up, and when I'd finished I'd rest and take my moon bath in the fountain.

"I spent about a year like this. And during that year of little chores and big chores, I hardly realized that the garden door didn't open any longer, and the moonbeam had stopped coming in. But what difference did that make? I had another pathway, which I loved because I'd had such a hard time making it . . . As for the moon . . . frankly, it'd been a while now since I'd been there, always bogged down with work, busy, worn out. And I hardly remembered where the poplars with one-sided leaves stood, or where the pairs of ermines were, or the starched lawns with white blackbirds. But all this . . . I thought one day or another I'd go back there, calmly, and stroll along the flour walk and chat with the bakers' souls . . . And the night I decided to go, and believe me I'd rather not talk about it because it's so sad . . . the night I decided I left the scissors and rope in the toolbox and, dressed up from head to toe, I started climbing up the shaft. And I don't know why, perhaps because that's what happens to dreams, that when you're not even thinking about them someone comes along who doesn't know anything and crushes them . . . I found the shaft cut in the middle, all the strands dangling loosely from above. Between my piece and the higher one, which hung like the hair of a drowned woman I saw once when I was a child and they were pulling her out of the river, there wasn't even a speck of light I could use as a stepping stone. I went back down as fast as I could. I got into bed and stayed there all the next day. I still don't know how I kept from going crazy. My temples were pounding, and my heart thumped against my chest like a rock bouncing around in a box.

"At nightfall, from my kitchen window, I saw the strands all lying on the ground around the fountain. I don't know where I found the strength to go out. I laid out the strands, I wanted to lift them up, but I couldn't get them even two feet off the ground. To give myself courage, I started singing the song about every night, every night, every night. But it didn't cheer me up at all, and the strands stayed piled up around the fountain. I didn't even have to pick them up, because the third night they disappeared. When I'd lost all hope, I got dressed up again one night and towards dawn, because it was hard for me to work myself up to it, I went out for a turn around the garden. I was a shadow of what I had been. I went back the next day, and the next and the next . . . The door was always shut and the moon, on the clear nights, spread its beams and lit up the broken glass on top of the walls and the window-panes along the gallery. One evening, while I was strolling and thinking about the work I'd do the next day, the garden door opened without a squeak from its hinges, like a dead door. I hardly breathed. A knife was piercing my heart. And the moonbeam entered and slid up to my feet. And I stamped on it furiously one, two, three times. But it didn't even move, and at the third stamp I realized I was walking and it seemed like I went from pain to unbearable delight. And the knife in my heart was melting, like it was made of ice and surrounded by warm blood . . . I went slowly, majestically upwards.

"And all at once I got to the spot where, now that I think about it honestly, it seems like the place where everyone one time or another . . . In brief, the beam stopped short at a black precipice. And I saw the great beast of nighttime, gnawing his tail in the depths of his vast, dark convulsions. High above there was a speck of light, which seemed like the shadow's restlessness . . . Resigned, I turned around, and very carefully started down again. Sadness, which never cheats, had cheated me. Everything was finished. The kindly light had opened up a last pathway of hope, but that pathway was blocked. I longed to turn around and look back, but I didn't dare. I didn't have the heart to. I was thinking, now you'll fall, now you'll fall, now you'll fall . . .

"When I got to the bottom, I entered the garden and bolted and locked the door. And here you have me. All moon and pain. And if I've told you about my earlier happiness, maybe it's because I needed to hurt myself a little more. But above all, to finish killing my secret, because a told secret is a dead secret. Between the two of us, we've been killing it little by little, with me talking and you listening. And here I am, like some big clumsy oaf, not knowing where I got this wooden spool in my hand. And this thing I've spent so many hours pondering . . . with my face all white, with my skin all white, a bit scorched and pock-marked because the moon lives on that kind of thing . . . And every day I'm more convinced that I've never been to the moon, that the man from the fountain who looked so much like me, who would have resembled me so very much if they'd taken all the joy out of him, and the laughs I had with the night beneath the shaft made of silk and flowers, and the little seeds splitting in half, they never existed . . . There's nothing left inside me. Only the sad things everyone has inside them. Yes. Only the sad things that stay inside you, lying flat like corpses under the earth. Cemeteries and cemeteries . . . Inside the earth. Yessir. Inside the earth."

A White Geranium Petal

BALBINA DIED on a warm night, between the last stars and the fog that rose from the sea. I had to open the dining room balcony, which looked out on the yard and made a cross-current with the windows facing the street, because as soon as Balbina passed away, death filled the whole house with its smell of rotting flowers. While she was dying, I sat in a low chair, keeping watch over her by candlelight. I'd been watching her like that ever since she got sick. Every night till I fell asleep. I'd lie down beside her fever, and look at her almond-streaked eyes. They watched me without watching me, shining like cat's eyes in the dark. I felt like the heat from that long sickness kept me company. By keeping the house shut up for so long, it'd made everything damp and peeled the wallpaper. Balbina's cheeks were hollow when she died. The tops of her hands were bony, and her knees had lost those dimples that had been my downfall. And I sucked in her final breath, lying on top of her, when her eyes were already bulging from suffocation, to steal the scrap of life she had left, which I wanted for myself. And with that finished life in my mouth, I went to throw open the balcony doors when I realized death wasn't going to leave.

There was a kind of magic in the yard, of sun and fog, and between that magic and me, a white geranium petal floated down. We kept the red geraniums, which were mine, by the railing which faced the street. And by the railing which faced the yard, the white ones which were Balbina's. As I watched that geranium petal, I remembered all the months of waiting for Balbina to die, always looking to see if her eyes were closing from sleepiness so I could wake her up. Because to finish her off faster, I didn't let her sleep. As soon as I heard her breathing a little more peacefully, I'd get up very slowly, go over to the wardrobe, climb up on the middle chair, and pick up the trumpet I kept hidden on top.

One morning a while back, while I was putting the curls on a marble angel, a tall woman came in, very thin, with a long nose and dried-out lips. She was wearing a hat with a bird on it, which she'd stuck clumsily on her head. A little boy in a sailor suit was holding her hand, clutching to his chest a shiny golden trumpet, decorated with tassles and red cords. The woman had come to order a grey marble tombstone for her husband's grave. Above the name and words, she wanted three white marble chrysanthemums, standing upright side-by-side: the first a little taller and the third a little shorter than the one in the middle. She wanted it right away. My boss told her I'd forget about the angel and do the tombstone immediately, but not with the chrysanthemums sticking out, as if they'd been left on top of the marble, but engraved in it and tied together in a bouquet. But after she left he said the angel was the most important thing, that the angel came first. And I went on doing the curls. Every evening when I got home, I'd tell Balbina I was making an angel all by myself, because my boss once told her I was a bad marble worker and he couldn't give me a whole figure to make. And that day with the woman and her chrysanthemums, at closing time I noticed the boy had left his trumpet at the foot of a kneeling figure. And I took it away with me because it was so lovely, all red and gold. So Balbina wouldn't ask me where I'd gotten it, I hid it on top of the wardrobe and forgot all about it. Till one night when Balbina was sleeping, to punish her for her sins, I pulled the chair over to the wardrobe, climbed up, picked up the trumpet in the dark and blew into it a little, very softly. I blew harder and made that sound, half moan, half shriek of sadness, half music from heaven. I heard Balbina stirring, put the trumpet back on top of the wardrobe, and very carefully got into bed. And after that day, from then on, when Balbina was sound asleep I'd play moans on the trumpet. The first time I did it, I waited for Balbina to wake up the next morning, dying from holding back my laughter, thinking she'd tell me about the strange sound that had half-woken her up in the night. But she never said she'd heard the trumpet. And I watched her back while she was coming and going between the dining room and the kitchen. I thought maybe if I looked daggers just above her spine, I'd discover her secret thoughts, in that place where the brain has another little brain that gathers and keeps all our secrets.

And then she got sick. Always in bed, always lying in bed, with that thin voice whining "I'm tired, I'm tired." And one night when I was watching her and listening to her quiet breathing, the way trees are supposed to breathe, she suddenly opened her mouth, stuck out the tip of her tongue, and made a sound like a trumpet with her tongue and lips. What I'd been patiently putting in her ears had come out of her mouth. And when she'd been dead for a while it seemed like her sunken cheeks filled out and her lips became young again and her body seemed to be resting . . . This whole miracle be-

fore I could go over and open the door to the balcony that
looked out on the yard. And while this change was happening
I noticed the cat, lying at the foot of the bed. He'd seen me suck
Balbina's last breath, and I grabbed him by the throat and
threw him across the room. A minute later he was back again
at the foot of the bed, lying there as if he'd never even moved. I
dressed her while she was still warm. I took off all her clothes,
the ones she'd been wearing ever since she got sick. They
made her look ugly, but I wouldn't let her change them, even
to sleep. And suddenly I stopped, enchanted by her delicate
white legs. I stroked her knee with my hand, round and round
the kneecap, and the cat must have thought I was playing because he stuck out his paw and touched my fingers. When I'd
dressed her and combed her hair, I closed her eyes and folded
her hands on top of her breast. One of them I had to open,
because it was shut tight. And finally, with a lot of trouble,
which for some reason was mixed with a crazy joy, I slowly
shut her mouth.

I went out, and I thought the cat had stayed behind with her,
but he must have followed me. Because when that geranium
petal was falling, he sat up on his hind legs to catch it before it
reached the ground. But I was taller and grabbed it in midair,
and the petal seemed like a milktooth. It had a milktooth smell:
the same smell as Balbina's mouth the first time we slept together. And when I realized what I was doing I already had the
pincers in my hand, I was already beside Balbina and was pulling out one of her upper teeth, a tooth so hard and so firmly
rooted that when it gave it felt like her whole jaw was coming
out. I took it in my hand. It was clean, and I licked it to get the
red off around the root. I put it in my pocket. The cat watched
everything, and after that day I never called him by his name
anymore, which was Mishu. From then on I called him Cosme,
because Mishu was what Balbina had christened him when

Cosme gave him to her. And when I'd decided to call him Cosme, I lifted dead Balbina's skirt, respectfully, with great respect, and rubbed her belly over and over again with my finger, like I had nothing else to do, from the bellybutton down. And when I thought it was time for Cosme to leave his house to go to work, I pulled Balbina's skirt down and went out into the street, with the cat behind me, and I told Cosme she was dead. He turned white as a sheet, because he'd been thinking about my Balbina for the longest time, and she'd never been and never would be his. His blood had lost its redness and turned to water. Because he and Balbina were in love with each other.

And when the gravediggers came and welded the coffin lid shut with their blowtorches, I thought this must be hell. On the way back from the burial, I went into a tavern to have a glass of wine and steady myself. And when I left the tavern, all full of red wine and with Balbina's tooth in my pocket, the blue dream started to come to me. And it followed me into my house. The cat rubbed his belly against my legs and got in my way, and I gave him a good kick. The moon, the stars, the water from the tap, everything was blue. And full of the dream, I sat down on the table and talked to the cat. I told him that soon Balbina'd be nothing but bones. For the burial, I'd dressed her in her new pink outfit. She'd made it so Cosme would fall in love with her, and now it'd be full of bones within a year, the same color as a marble angel with outstretched wings and well-combed curls. I showed him the tooth. He looked at it, closed his eyes, and his whiskers stiffened. He had honey-colored eyes with black stripes down the middle, cutting the honey in half. After a while he looked at the tooth again, and every night I'd show him the tooth. But one day he stuck out his paw. I'd bent over to show him the tooth close up, and suddenly his paw shot out and the tooth fell on the floor and rolled into a corner. I had trouble finding it, and I stuck the cat in a sack and beat him. Then I made a hole in the tooth, and put a thick string through the hole. And I always played with the cat, showing him the tooth and throwing it up in the air when he stuck out his paw to touch it. Playing and playing, one day he opened his mouth and swallowed it. There was still a piece of string hanging out, and I managed to calm him down by talking gently to him. And when he was calmed down I pulled the string to get the tooth out. But the string, which was frayed and soaked with spit, finally broke. And the tooth stayed inside the cat Cosme'd given Balbina when it was just a kitten, who followed her around the house, in the yard, and on the terrace.

I went out in the street to have a look at the blue stars, frantic over having lost the tooth. The cat stayed beside me, looking up at the sky just like I was. I put him in the house and locked the door, and started walking, and while I was walking I kept saying "Cosme loved Balbina, Cosme loved Balbina and now Balbina's dead and let her stay dead, I like it, I like it, I like it." And he'd never had the chance to hold her, because between the two of them there was a marble worker who put curls on angels and played a hidden trumpet to drive Balbina crazy and kill her little by little so he could bury her without her tooth, in that pink outfit she'd made one spring because Cosme had a pink geranium in his window facing the street. And so he'd see her walking by on Sundays, wearing a very thin veil dotted with black sequins.

I bought a fish all covered with scales, and ate it fried with tomato and parsley. I gave the head to the cat. And I made him swallow the hard, thick central spine the wrong way, so the bones would prick him if he wanted to bring it up. And immediately he started shaking and shaking to get the spine out, and the more he shook the more the spine stuck in his throat's pink flesh. And a few days later, from so much trying to get that spine out and from so much dry heaving, his soul left his body, and still warm, like when I'd dressed Balbina, I slit him from top to bottom with a razorblade. And I found the tooth, white as ever, in a corner of his puffed-up gut. I washed it with soap and rubbed it for a long time with my finger to get it shiny again.

That night I went out to bury the cat. I went out every night, to see if I was still seeing those blue stars. I went past the end of the paved street to where there were streetlamps but no houses, and some miserable gardens with cabbages eaten by caterpillars and rues all full of plant lice. And the light from the streetlamps without houses was blue too. I ended up thinking everything was blue, not because I was seeing it blue but because it'd turned blue. And I asked this or that person what color the stars were, and what color they thought the moon was when they saw it straight and when they saw it with a ring around it. And all of them, after looking at me for a while as if I'd asked some really strange question, told me the stars were the same color as a lightbulb and so was the moon. And the tap water was just water-colored, and nothing more.

And I went on chipping away at the marble. My boss had finished the angel and I was done with the curls. The tombstone was ready, and I was putting the folds on a skirt for a girl who was laid out dead. The first few came out crooked, and the boss told me "You're even worse now that your wife's dead . . ." The night after he told me that I went farther than the other nights – past the gardens, past where I'd buried the cat, past the cabbages and the rues. The last streetlamp was blue and I kept throwing stones at it, aiming for the blue light. The night was dark. After throwing stones for hours, I finally hit the bulb and it fell in little pieces. Then I sat down against the lamppost, alone facing the dark night. And then, when the first star came out and the house windows in the distance were all black, out of the darkness and the smell from the fields came a meow, and then another, closer and closer, and without a sound, a shadow came out of a clump of tall grass. And the shadow came up to me. It was an enormous cat, as big as three cats put together. And his pupils, which I thought maybe would look blue, were honey-colored, like old honey, split from top to bottom by a black stripe. The cat walked by, rubbing his belly against my knees, three or four times because he was circling around the lamppost. I got up and started for home. He followed me, but when I got to the first gardens I turned around and I found he'd disappeared. The next day, while I was chipping at the skirt folds for that girl who was laid out dead and constantly spitting out marbledust, besides thinking of the blue light, I also thought about the streetlamp without a bulb and the cat.

And as soon as it was dark, I went back to the last streetlamp. You could hear a gang of ragged, crazy roosters crowing. The fat cat came back. He didn't come from the vacant lots and the high grass. I found him in front of me, with his honey eyes fixed on mine, blacker than the dark night of the soul. And every night he came. I sat against the lamppost. I waited a while, as the wind blew away the fallen leaves. And all of a sudden, I found him right next to me, quiet, like he was made of stone. I got in the habit of showing him Balbina's tooth. When he saw it, he'd rub against my legs, purring all the time, and he'd look at the tooth with those bees' honey eyes of his. And the last night I found him waiting for me, I took the tooth out of my pocket and bounced it around in the palm of my hand. But without even looking at it, he started circling around the lamppost like a rope. And each time he went around he'd tie me to the lamp and, tying and tying, he bound me tighter and tighter till I felt like he was binding my life forever. And my thoughts went out past the gardens, on the path to the cemetery, and came back but not all the way back, between the fields and the streetlamp without a bulb. I looked at the darkness in front of me, to see if it was getting blue, blue from side to side and from top to bottom. And with that noose around my neck, and my tongue half out, I saw it turn blue and delicate, like those stars Balbina had embroidered on a table-cloth. Because Balbina was an embroideress, and besides em-broidering blue stars she embroidered letters that looked like leaves and branches on sheets and pillowcases, and the blue-ness of the night was blue like those stars made of thread. Blue, blue like Balbina's eyes, who when I met her was called the blue-eyed girl, and afterwards I'd forgotten she even had them.

The Sea

THEY WALKED SLOWLY. The taller one was a solemn man,
well-dressed, with a grey beard and reddish cheeks. The other, skinny and unshaven, looked as if he'd just recovered from
an illness. They were engrossed in conversation, and the taller
one would stop from time to time, stroking his beard as if he
wanted to weigh his words carefully.

"One hasn't time for everything in life. To laugh and to cry,
be amused and bored. And as soon as you're born you have to
prepare for death. That's why babies cry, because they already
smell it."

"Already smell what?"

"The scent of death . . . Afterwards, one gets used to it . . .
You know what fills me with respect? To think there's an aircraft carrier behind Montjuïc. You see? . . . When I was young I
would have liked to serve on an aircraft carrier. Did you ever
see a film with an aircraft carrier in it?"

"I saw one years ago, with two planes that were coming

back with their engines on fire. And one of the planes, the second one, crashed into the guy who was giving signals with those little flags . . . But the strangest thing was . . ."

"He must have died."

"Who?"

"The guy with the flags."

"Instantly. For me the strangest thing, as I was saying . . ."

"The strangest thing of all is that submarine mystery. Do you remember?"

"Yes, but . . ."

"What are you looking at?"

"That slate-colored cloud . . . That submarine stuff was a joke."

"If all those complications were a joke . . . Look, if I were rich and one of them came through I'd want to be on it. If the Mau-Maus made trouble, I'd be there. And by Mau-Maus I mean any adventure. Because without adventure . . . But you wouldn't, as far as I can see. You'd say it's a joke and by now we've got it under control and you'd be all set to go to sleep with a long nightshirt down to your toes. You never think."

"I like to sit facing the sea and keep perfectly still. You can't sleep in peace with that restlessness in your soul."

"Restlessness is life. The sea, look at it calmly, it doesn't say anything to me. The aircraft carrier on top of it I find interesting . . ."

"So to you it's like the seashells were forming?"

"What do you mean?"

"The shells are made by the sea. And without the sea that aircraft carrier you're so fond of would need wheels. Don't you see? The sea is the world's greatest mystery. Take a good look at it."

"You're always saying look, look, look . . ."

"You too. Look: you're on the north pole and I'm on the

south pole. To me the sea, with this uneasiness of the waves, is a tragedy."

"Tap water with a little salt in it."

"Water so deep it never ends, and what goes on inside it . . ."

"Fishes that come and go . . ."

"Beneath it there are sunken cities and men. I can't look at this restless water without feeling altered from top to bottom. And the foam . . . millions and millions of little bubbles made by the waves. This water which is neither blue nor green, with broken sun and broken sky, is full of barges that the tap water, as you put it, swallowed in one gulp . . ."

"And you say you feel empty when you look at the sea . . . You sure mull things over."

"The dead things bother me. And the living ones astonish me."

"Frankly, the sea leaves me cold. Now if the sea brings a revolution like the submarine, then I'm as hot as a boiler. Let's sit down on this bench."

They sat down on the bench. A woman was already sitting there, holding a cage in her lap with a goldfinch in it. She was just holding the cage, while she fed bits of lettuce to the bird which, after looking at the woman very carefully, would take them from between the metal bars. When the two men sat down the woman moved over, gathering up her skirts to make room for them. The tall man took a sheaf of newspaper clippings out of his pocket.

"See? I brought all the clippings. Here, read this. See if you still dare to say it's a joke. Wait a minute. I've got them arranged, but I looked at them before coming and I think they're out of order. Things get mixed up by themselves. When you're not thinking . . . Excuse me. A little patience is always a good thing. Let's see. The joke, as you say, begins on the 12th . . . 15th . . . Look . . . You see? You've infected me now with your look, look . . . Good, let's get down to work. The first articles I don't have because I was preoccupied with other things . . . but I started saving them on the day when the so-called decisive battle began. The whole sea, around the area where they thought the submarine was, was covered by airplanes. Airplanes all over, and the submarine lurking as far below the surface as it could get. The chicken."

"Look."

"What is it?"

"Those kids looking at the sea."

They were a boy and a girl. The boy must have been about seven. He was wearing long pants and a wine-colored sweater with holes in the elbows and a high neck. The girl couldn't have been more than three, and was stuffed into a red skirt that was half-twisted and a purple sweater. Neither of them wore shoes. The setting sun nailed their long, slender shadows to the ground.

"Let them be. The submarine, very closely watched, is determined to surface. From the shore you could see how the Argentine expeditionary force was attacking the submarine."

"And the planes?"

"Listen carefully to what I say. The headline says the United States won't help . . . the Argentines attack."

"But what was the submarine looking for?"

"First of all, it seems like it wanted to surface to charge its batteries."

"And why didn't they let it charge them?"

"The first thing it wanted was to come up for air. And then they tried to close the gulf."

"And did they manage to close it?"

"I don't know. The papers say so. You think the Argentines had no plan of action?"

"I don't know."

"Then shut up and listen. While they were attacking, in Buenos Aires they arrested three other people mixed up in the affair, and they seized a radio operator on the Patagonian border who was communicating with the submarine by means of a two-way radio. It seems this operator gave all kinds of explanations, that he was studying the weather, etc. etc., but once they found his message they made him read it to them word-for-word, so that he couldn't keep on denying it and they put him in jail."

"And what did the message say?"

"No one knows. Wait a minute. The 16th . . the 19th . . . Now we're back to the 14th . . . Let me look for the 18th. The 18th clears up a lot of things."

While the tall man was arranging the newspaper clippings, his friend turned to the woman.

"Have you had it long?"

"You mean the goldfinch?"

"Yes."

"The little darling's very old. See what long claws she has?"

"I thought so. Not from the claws, which I didn't see, but from the way she looked at you. She looks very wise . . . and she eats the lettuce as if she were choosing the tenderest pieces."

"She thinks they're slips of paper."

The tall man, who by now had arranged the clippings, gave his friend a nudge with his elbow.

"Listen. The 12th . . . strange submarine in Argentine waters . . . and then . . . Look, here's the 13th . . . Wait."

"What do you mean, slips of paper?"

The boy and girl had stopped watching the sea. They'd come over to the bench, and were fascinated by the goldfinch.

"Lottery slips. I run a lottery for the girls ... For their dreams, with pink slips and blue slips ... In the municipal markets. Always about love."

"Be so good as to leave this woman alone ... The 13th: three persons arrested with radio. The 14th: submarine found to be Russian. Argentines reinforced with U.S. arms ... Remember how the headlines said there wouldn't be U.S. aid? And it says the submarine could escape if it wanted to ..."

"Didn't it say the gulf was closed?"

"Yes. Wait a minute ... the 15th: frogman discovered. It says no frogman can weigh more than a hundred and fifty pounds. Or be over five and a half feet tall. The 16th ... where's the 16th ... where are you hiding, 16th?"

"Don't get upset. Did you ever see such a pretty goldfinch?"

"Goldfinch? Where?"

"The woman next to me."

"Oh, here's the 16th. Leave the goldfinch alone and listen to me. It says the Argentines, helped by the Americans, the North Americans, were just about to attack ... The blue and white and the stars and stripes. And now in Port Meyrin there's ..."

"That didn't come up before."

"What?"

"That name."

"Don't talk nonsense. It says they deny there was a frogman in Port Meyrin. And under the column with the denial there's another column that says four frogmen are searching for the submarine. And furthermore it says a storm is making the search difficult because, with the clouds and the thunder ..."

"The sea is ruled by the moon, and the moon gives the orders."

"Oh, you're interested in the moon too?"

It was the woman with the goldfinch, who'd been listening to them for a while now. The girl brought her finger up to the cage and without touching it started to laugh. The boy grabbed her hand and pulled it away.

"Leave the moon alone."

"My godson, who's coming for me on his motorcycle, always says he'd like to be the first man on the moon."

"We're talking about a submarine . . . Now we go to the 18th: it says they're almost certain the story about the dead frogman was false."

"Didn't it say there were four of them?"

"Yes. First it said one and then four, but on the 18th they deny finding a dead frogman. And it says the submarines are still in the gulf and – here they are – that the frogmen, if the submarines . . ."

"Up to now they were only talking about one submarine."

"If you don't mind . . . Sometimes they play down a news item so as not to excite the public."

"But if they were talking about just one frogman in the beginning, and one submarine, why do they suddenly come up with more frogmen and more submarines?"

"What do you want me to say? That you're right, you who possibly don't even know where Argentina is, and please forgive me? Do me the favor of listening, or if not, then let's stop."

"Perhaps that would be better . . ."

". . . and it says the four frogmen, if the submarines don't obey orders to surrender – which Radio Argentina and the Americans are constantly broadcasting – they'll lay four mines, two on each side, even if it kills them. And listen to this, now it says that without further hesitation the submarines . . . In the plural. So there were several of them."

"I don't understand how a person like you . . ."

"What does that mean – a person like me? That I'll swallow anything?"

"Not anything, just whoppers."

"If you think you're being nice . . ."

"Don't get angry, my good man, don't get angry. Let me hear the end of the story. I'm listening."

"I'm listening, I'm listening . . . All that's left now is the bombshell story, as they say. See? On the first page there's a banner headline: submarine attacked with depth charges. And it also says some swimming champions have offered to help the frogmen. And it says they're working together, on the first night of the new moon."

The woman with the goldfinch nodded her head, with her eyes slightly shut.

"When my godson comes, he'll tell you how much he wants to go to the moon. At night he studies about rockets."

"And why don't you go to the moon yourself?"

"If I were my godson's age . . . Did you know that on a rocket you float and your food floats and you live all upside down?"

The boy laughed and said to the woman: "Can we take the goldfinch for a walk?"

"What did you say?"

"My sister would like to take the goldfinch for a walk. Just a little way. Holding onto the handle."

"No, she's very delicate and she'd get frightened."

"What does the boy want?"

"He says his sister wants to take the goldfinch for a walk, and the lady doesn't want her to."

"Leave them be and listen. We're coming to the end now. What is it with you and that goldfinch? It says finally there are only two embassies that haven't told the Argentine government whether the submarines are theirs or not. By now we can guess which ones. And the submarines are playing hide-and-seek and the search party doesn't know what to do."

"That's all just a tale made up to distract people from the rockets and the moon."

"You think so, eh? You, who spend hours gazing at the waves and thinking how seashells are made, you think it's important to send a rocket to the moon, when from what they tell us they don't even know if it gets there."

"My godson says if they could put space stations around the moon we'd never be hot or cold again."

"Your godson would be better off working."

"It's clear that you two don't work for a living. Every afternoon you come here to waste time. Today you saw me because you walked a little further and sat down on my bench. But I see you every day. If you knew what troubles I've had . . ."

"Look, your life story . . ."

"An evil vision came to me while I was looking at the plum tree. After washing the dishes . . ."

"Leave us alone."

"Be quiet, she's not hurting anyone."

"In the evening, I'd always lean out the kitchen window so I could look at the plum tree down below. It hurt me to see it, because it lived in the garden of an abandoned house and nobody watered it and all winter I was wondering if it would still be alive in the spring."

"You or the plum tree?"

"The plum tree. And when winter was over I couldn't sleep in peace till the buds appeared and its blood started breathing again. One night I went blind, totally blind. I couldn't see the plum tree or the streetlights or the sky above – only black and more black. I stood up quickly, with my nose full of the scent of danger, and then from far away, out of the blackness, a ghost-like figure came towards me, wrapped in a loose sheet that moved like the flame on a candle when you pass in front of it. It had two black holes for eyes, as if they were cut out of paper, and the black was the black that filled everything. And then when I was just about dying of fright, it vanished. I thought: now he's dead. He's been killed in the war. But that wasn't it. It was a warning. A warning came to me."

"What came to you?"

"My husband. Isn't it sad how I have to come here every afternoon to wait for my godson, so that if he feels like it he can take me home and let me sleep in his house? . . . The fear coiled round my insides like an evil snake . . . I closed the kitchen window, and I never looked at that plum tree again after dinner."

"You didn't say you stayed blind, did you?"

"Only while I saw the vision. It was a warning that my husband, who'd gone off with the Blue Divisions,* and whom everybody'd given up for dead, had come back. After so many years! And I can't get rid of him. He wants to live with me, he really wants to live with me."

"Lock him out."

"Say you don't want him."

"That's what I did, but I found him lying on the landing waiting for me to get home from work. That first day in the darkness, so that I tripped on the stairs and almost fell down them . . . I had him hidden in the attic all during the Civil War, since we lived alone in the house. And I brought him food that I took out of my own mouth. And him hiding in his corner, thinking only of the men from the political committee. Afterwards it was just our luck that he ended up in the Blue Divisions. And when he'd been gone for years and I thought he'd

---

*Translator's note: The Blue Divisions were Spanish "volunteers" who participated in the Nazi invasion of Russia.

frozen to death in the snow he comes back. Old and dirty, and right away he asks about our daughter Carlota, who died of pneumonia when she was fifteen, and he puts the blame on me. And when I tell him I don't want him he lies down in front of me on the landing. And every day he knocks on the door when he knows I'm at home. I open it with the chain, look around, and shut it without saying a word. And he starts knocking again. I act like I don't hear, but he keeps coming back. And inside I'm going crazy. I don't know what to do. And then one day, when I've got the door open on the chain, he tells me through the crack that he'll pick the lock and chop the goldfinch's head off. And how he'll throw me out of bed and make me sleep on the floor."

The girl had opened the door to the cage some time ago, and the goldfinch had gotten out. For a moment it stood quietly on the woman's skirt. Then it hopped to the ground and started strutting around with the two children behind it.

"You lost your goldfinch while you were telling us about your husband."

"Who let her out?"

"Who do you think? Those kids who wanted to take it for a walk."

The woman stood up, white as a sheet.

"Try and catch it!"

"And how would you like us to catch it? You always come up with such great plans!"

"Could you tell the children to come back?"

"Children, come back!"

"Watch out for the cars, make sure they don't crush it. Maybe it'll come back soon."

"I think you've seen the last of it."

"Oh, the poor darling . . . Now she's on the railing. You see how she flies, and just last week I clipped her wings."

"Instead of talking about rockets and the moon and your husband's shenanigans, you should have kept an eye on those two."

"Yes, you're right, but she likes the sound of the sea. Can't you see she's totally lost and doesn't even hear me? . . . Somebody catch her! There's my godson coming through the rocks."

The two men stood in the middle of the path with their arms outstretched. The godson slammed on his brakes just in front of the first one. He turned the motorcycle around, parked it, and very casually asked what was going on. The woman told him that the goldfinch, stunned by the noise of the water, was about to throw itself into the sea. Then he went over to the girl, took the cage away from her, tore off the door, and showed the cage to the goldfinch, which was watching everything out of the corner of its eye and, half-crouching, tried to keep as far away as possible. The goldfinch took a hop and turned to face them, with its head cocked and its eyes round as a chicken's, then opened its wings and closed them again. Then it rested for a moment, listening. Suddenly, it shook its tail, ruffled its breast feathers, pecked at its breast a few times, and fluttered to the ground. Then it walked into the cage.

"She went in like a real lady."

The godson looked at the woman, who kept saying "like a real lady, like a real lady." Then he came up behind the cage and, covering the door with one hand, lifted it off the ground.

"Here, take it, and next time be more careful."

"It was those kids who were fooling with it while I was talking about the moon with these two gentlemen who were talking about the sea. And the door?"

"I'll put it back on."

He took hold of her arm and led her towards the motorcycle. When the woman was about to get on, the two children both started crying at the same time. The two men, who also were leaving, stopped.

"Let them cry," the godson said.

But the woman came up to them with the cage and asked them why they were crying, and the little boy said they were lost and didn't know the way home. Then the tall man's newspaper clippings fell to the ground, and he bent over to pick them up.

"What did they say?"

"They're lost."

The godson asked them if they lived nearby. He'd taken a handkerchief out of his pocket, and was wiping the tears and mucus from the girl's face. The boy said he didn't know. They'd wanted to look at the sea, and when their mother found out they weren't at home she'd try to kill herself, since she was always trying to kill herself, no matter what they did, and she'd also tried to kill herself one day when they went to look at the flower stalls and his little sister who didn't know any better had grabbed a broken flower that the florist-lady had thrown on the ground because she couldn't use it in the bouquet she was making. That night their mother got sick and tossed around a lot in her sleep and each time she moved she'd wake them up because they were sleeping right next to her. The woman with the goldfinch asked him what his father did, what his job was, and he said he didn't have a father but the girl had two, a soldier and a clerk, who were always giving them chocolate-covered hazelnuts. While the boy was talking, the girl had opened one of her hands and without saying anything showed them a sequin she'd taken from her skirt pocket, and the woman said "Look what she's showing us," and the boy explained how it had fallen off her mother's work uniform. And how she had another, scarlet, with frills around the bottom, and when she wore it and sang her mother pretended she was a carnation dying of thirst. And one time she showed them how she could lean over till she was lying on the ground. And the girl twirled around.

"We'll have to take them to the police," said the tall man, having picked up his clippings.

"Why the police?"

"So they can find out where they live."

"Did you hear that? They say they live at the foot of a mountain."

"There's no other solution. We'll have to take them to the police."

The godson said he'd take care of it, and went towards the motorcycle with a child on each hand and the woman behind them. They climbed on as best they could. The godson grabbed the handle-bars, started the engine with a kick, turned the motorcycle around, and with a great roar they all drove off together.

"What do you think of that?"

"What do *you* think? A woman who shows her legs, some lost children, a lady who sees visions . . . When I think how well the afternoon began . . ."

"Look, let their mother show whatever she likes. It's all the same to me. But she should keep them locked up at home. If she lets them wander around in the streets, they'll be urchins within a few years, and instead of opening a little cage they'll steal your wallet."

"Whose wallet?"

"Yours."

"And why mine?"

"I mean anybody's. And as for that woman with the gold-finch, there was a moment there when I would have loved to bash her one. And besides, if her husband did go off to fight in the snow, it was so that you and I could live in peace. You have to get to the bottom of things."

"You always want to get to the bottom of things. To the bottom of the sea. I see them too, the ghost towns with fish in the streets. And the seashells being born. But I can't see how there can be any mystery in a mussel."

"Why not? Don't you see it in life?"

"Even in oysters, with those pearls they make. But to tell you the truth I find more life in an internal-combustion engine than in a carrot. Not to mention shellfish. Down there guzzling sand, with the water endlessly washing over them . . ."

"Don't be such an idiot . . ."

"When you eat them, what do you find inside?"

The tall man stopped walking, and gazed at the other for a moment in silence, with his hand on his beard.

"We've known each other for a while now, and basically we agree. You like the natural sciences, and I like mechanical things. And by the way, where are the chestnuts?"

"What chestnuts?"

"The ones we bought when we were coming, to eat on the bench . . . Didn't you put them in your raincoat pocket?"

"No. You're the one who's been holding them."

"Then I've lost them. Maybe the children took them. In any case, they wouldn't be any good cold. Do you want to go buy some more?"

"And tell the chestnut lady about the submarine. That'll make her jaw drop."

"Maybe she'll tell us her husband's just been strangled to death, or that he's got leprosy. I'm fed up with other people's troubles . . . look how angry it is . . ."

"What?"

"The sea."

"It must be sick of hearing us."

"And I'm sick of hearing the waves. Think of that radio operator in Patagonia, so peaceful . . ."

"And surrounded by spies. You really believe all that stuff?"

"It's what the papers say."

"Come on, let's go. Got everything?"

And they left without saying a word. Soon they began to run because it had started raining.

My Christina

"YOU LIVED inside for so many years? How did you do it? You'd better get your papers straightened out." And they look at me, and I see the laughter starting at the corners of their mouths. "Come back," they say, "come back." But when I do come back they tease me. "Come tomorrow, we still don't know, come the day after tomorrow." And one guy, the one with the mustache, sticks out his hand with the first two fingers together and makes like he's turning a key, and giving me a dirty look he says, "If you don't come for the papers, you know . . ." And he moves his hand . . . And inside the pain is killing me, but no one realizes it. That's how it went, without witnesses. And I'm not complaining.

The whole sea howling and roaring and the waves in ribbons and me caught and thrown, thrown and caught, spat out and swallowed, clutching my plank. Everything was black, the sea and the night, and the *Christina* sinking. You couldn't hear the cries of the drowning anymore. And the thought came to me that there was only one person still alive, and that was me, by the wonderful luck of being only a sailor and on deck when things started going wrong. I saw thick clouds without wanting to see them, lying flat on an angry wave, and then, with those clouds up above me, I felt myself sucked down, farther down than the other times. I went down among whirlpools and frightened fish that brushed against my cheeks, down and down, swept down a hill by some enormous underwater current. And when the water calmed down and started receding little by little, a fish bigger than the others smashed against my leg with his tail. And I didn't see any more clouds, just darkness. Darker than any mother's son had ever seen, and the plank saved me because without the plank maybe I'd have ended up all the way down at the bottom of that current. When I tried to get up and walk the ground slipped under me. I had an idea of where I was, but I didn't want to think about it, because I remembered what my mother said to me on her deathbed. I was standing beside the bed, very sad, and my mother, who was breathing her last, had the strength to sit halfway up, and with her arm, dry and long as a broomstick, she slapped my face hard and shouted, in a voice I could barely understand, "Don't think!" And she was dead.

I bent over to touch the ground with my hand. It was slimy, and while I was touching it I heard something nearby, like a huge blast on a horn that gradually turned into a roar. And with roars and blasts, like the wheezing of tired old lungs, the ground tilted upwards and I fell sitting down, clutching my plank. I was punch-drunk. I really didn't know what was happening. I only knew I had to hang onto that plank for dear life, because wood is stronger than water. In rough waters a plank is stronger than anything. I wanted to know exactly where I was, and when the side of my head stopped hurting so much I tried to walk. Everything was the color of ink from a frightened octopus, and the blasts had stopped and all you could hear was glug-glug, glug-glug. And the ground beneath my feet, because now I was standing up again, was like soft rubber, the kind that flows gently out of treetrunks. Rubber that's collected, worked, and dried, and then softened by heat from the sun. But inside I felt cold, and my teeth were chattering. My mind wandered, and I found myself sitting on the floor again, with the plank across my legs. I stretched out my arm and touched a wall. My hand was flat against it, and the whole wall moved like an endless wave, like some ancient restlessness. I picked up the plank just as it was falling, and stuck it against the moving wall, and the plank and I both sailed through the air and fell on the muddy floor and when it was firm I made a move forward. And so, with a lot of trouble, falling and picking myself up, I got to a strange place. It was dark, and at the same time full of colors that weren't really colors, blues and yellows and reds that flared up and died, coming closer and moving away, colors that weren't like colors. They were fiery but different from fire, indescribable, changing and fading away.

I saw a speck of light, a light that was pale and sickly, and I went towards it and saw the moon outside, coming through the whalebone. I let many hours go by, clutching my plank. I think. Because who knows where the time goes. And when the moon started going down, the colors became sort of rainbowlike and then I realized I wasn't breathing and water was coming out of my ears, a trickle down each side of my neck. But it wasn't water. It was blood, because my ears had burst inside, and as I was rubbing my finger over my neck which was warm from the blood, I felt a shudder coming from the bottom of where I was, and with the shudder a jet of water shot up, smelling like half-digested fish. And the water covered me up to my shoulders, and it was just by luck that it stopped there and little by little went down, but I still stank of fish all over. The blood had stopped flowing from my ears. Air went through them, because the airpath had changed. I rapped hard on the floor with the plank. Nothing happened, not one shudder or moan. I went forward, holding onto my plank, among colored lights, maybe the ones I'd already seen or maybe others, but slowly getting dimmer. And the light of dawn came through the whalebone, and I felt the calm seas' peace, something I can't describe, as if my world were about to fade away, I don't know . . . I stopped. Now that air was going through my ears, I could hear some enormous breathing, mixed with the splashing water. Then it seemed like I was constantly stepping on stones, but it was the bumps on a tongue, and suddenly the plank and I were tossed upward and I felt like something was giving me a big bearhug. The kind that takes your breath away. I'd half come out of a whale's spout, along with a lot of water. The plank had saved me from shooting straight up like a bullet. And I saw things I'd already seen many times, but from such a different angle! It was the largest whale in all the seas, the shiniest, the most ancient. I'd spent the whole night inside it.

The dawn came haltingly, and hanging from the bars in the opening to the spout, which by now were starting to hurt me, clutching my plank on the other side of the spout, with my feet swinging back and forth, I saw two rivers that flowed into the sea, very different from each other. The water in them had two colors: scarlet, like red earth, in one; and green, like seaweed, in the other. And those two colors made a peaceful dance, coming together and separating. Dancing and dancing the dance of colors. I'm scarlet, I'm all green. Now comes the scarlet, so the green drains away. Then the green trickles out at the bottom, so the scarlet disappears . . . And while I was watching, the sun came out. The hole got wider and I fell through it like a rock.

Then I saw what was inside. There was a sailor at the bottom, rocking to and fro in the water and spit. Stretched out flat on the tongue, within reach of me, his tie fastened with a little cord, an anchor on his sleeve, his pants sticking to his legs, his face purple, his eye sockets open and empty. Three fish were eating one of his hands. I scared them off but they came back, determined to keep on. I was hungry too, but I stood it, and holding my plank, I saluted the dead man and sang a hymn. I spent three days chasing fish and going from one side to the other, and from time to time the tongue would hit my face. Until . . . it's hard to say it . . . I spent those three days trying to get the sailor out. The whale ground its whalebone and I ground my teeth. I tightened my belt so I could put more force into it. So much belt-tightening made me hungry, and I started eating little pieces of the sailor. He was tough and stringy. Lots of sinew. I preferred eating an unknown sailor to one I'd met before. Some big fish had cleaned him out when he was still floating around in the water. He was all there, except for his eyes and guts. It had preserved him, and I was able to make him last some days. I tossed the small bones through the whalebone, but the bigger ones stayed there with me. The whalebone on the right side was stripped clean of scales. On the left it was a cluster of seaweed and shellfish and mussels. So I wouldn't always be eating sailor, I sometimes ate shellfish.

The worst thing was the thirst. But everything has its solution. And one day, by some miracle, a small ladle drifted in. I immediately thought of the rubber trees, and with one merciless shove, I rammed the handle into the whale's cheek. The next day it was full of fluid, and I could drink. It's the salt water in the sea that makes fish so tender. I rammed the handle in again. I always had to make new holes, because the wounds closed up right away. From time to time, if I didn't watch what

I was doing, she'd pin me against her cheek with her tongue and keep me there for hours and hours. Slowly we moved through the sea. By now I'd made several marks with my knife on a piece of whalebone. One morning I attacked the whalebone, to see if I could make a hole in it. Everything started spinning and I went up and down, sometimes on top of the tongue and sometime beneath it, sometimes to one side and sometimes above everything. And slammed up against the palate, I happened to yell out "Stop, Christina! . . ." I found myself sitting down, with the plank across my chest. And at that moment, without realizing it, I baptized the whale.

I saw all kinds of seas through the whalebone. Different blues and wine-colored. Anything you can imagine. Golden waves, and mountains of ice and mists at sunrise. And worrying and shivering, I told myself, "All the world's tears flow into the sea." And my clothes rotted and fell apart. First the bottoms of my pants got ragged, then my sailor shirt started fraying. I don't know how, but my clothes fell away, and I ended up with just my belt and my knife, with the mother-of-pearl handle stuck through the belt. Soon I had to make new holes in it. Sometimes when I was asleep, I'd dream I was tightening my belt and nothing was left inside it . . . Green shores! When I saw those shores I prayed. I came back to life and started pounding again with the plank. Christina dove. We stayed under for a long time. When we surfaced the circulation in my ears was all haywire. But the whalebone had opened like a floodgate, and I went out into God's sea which no longer seemed like tears but like laughter from all the fountains in the world. And I and my plank made our way through the sea, like this, from side to side, towards the green land. There were birds screaming above the water, and it seemed like the breeze brought smells of lavender and pine. But suddenly I felt her coming without even turning around, and she trapped me again in her whalebone mouth.

Then the real hell began. Six months, whole nights of pounding on the inside with the plank, banging her tongue with the sailor's legbone, and who knows where it would have ended. I took my knife and cut crosses in her cheeks' soft hollows, and under her tongue. I buried the handle of the ladle in her, which was rusty by now, to poison her blood. I punched holes in her with the belt buckle. In the end she wasn't even swimming. She drifted aimlessly on the surface, tilting a little to one side. I marked the days by burying the knife in her cheek. It shook like jelly, and blood and lymph flowed from the markings. When I'd carved up the whole inside of one cheek, I started marking the other one. One day I cut a bump off her tongue, and I heard a bellow. Like the organ on All Saints' Day. At night moans would come from deep inside her, as if all the bells in all the sea's belltowers were ringing at once, muffled by the depth of the water and the salt. Christina rocked like a cradle, and she rocked me to put me to sleep. But I never trusted her. I started eating her. I'd make a cross, and then cut the flesh beneath it and eat it well-chewed, like I'd done with the meat from the sailor. One day the moans seemed human. Christina dove. She spent a long time underwater. Even though I breathed through my ears, when we surfaced again it was like coming back from some watery hell. I cut her tonsil, I left the plank propped up at the entrance to her throat, and sliced lines in her tongue with my knife. Crosses and more crosses, days and more days. Sometimes I'd attack her cheek with the plank, in the spot where she had the least flesh left. Constantly. The tongue was too tough; I only ate her cheek. The flesh grew back, and I watched it grow like new spring grass ... When I stuck the bone from the sailor's leg under her tongue, she'd go out of her mind. But as soon as I left her in peace she'd start swimming again, tilting a little, slowly. As if the sea water, tired of her bouncing and howling, had grown thick and was hard to get through.

Time passed, with its days, its months, and its years. And we kept on moving forward, because deep inside we felt like, in some place we never managed to find, there awaited us – who knows what, the last bit of light on shadow, or one of those vague memories things leave when they fade away. At last I got tired. I lived huddled up in the hollow of a cheek, and she kept me there, pressing me lightly with her tongue, and I felt like she was packing me in and coating me with her drivel. And neither she nor I knew what seas we passed through. Till one night she ran aground on a rock, and on that rock she died. All marked up inside. The beach wasn't far away; barely half an hour by rowboat. I wanted to beat the whalebone open with my plank, but I couldn't because the plank by now was all rotten on the edges and had gotten shorter and thinner. With great pain I climbed out through the spout. When I was outside I slid down the enormous curve of her back till I reached the water. But I felt nothing, because I'd been living in a kind of limbo.

The sea tossed me onto the sand, and that's where they found me. I woke up in a hospital. A nun made me drink fresh milk. I couldn't swallow it, because my tongue and throat were like stone. And another nun with a little wooden mallet, which later they told me they'd had to have made specially, picked at the crust, which was like a pearl, and that's how they brought me around. At first the crust cracked with the hammering, and after some days it came off in flakes, because the nun had sprinkled it with a pitcher of special water. And the nun worked at it patiently and told me: "Sir, the skin under the crust looks like an earthworm." And when she had almost all the crust off, and there was only some left on my right cheek and in the middle of one side of my head, the nun gave me some pants and said I had to go down so they could make up my papers. So I went, and they asked me how I lived for so many years, and whether I really thought I was fooling them . . . And the wind and the sun, which sow and ripen, gave me a new skin, which was lucky because I was all raw like the hollow in Christina's cheek. And when I'd walked around enough I went back to the hospital, and the nun asked me if my thin skin hurt in the street. I told her it only hurt – a lot – when she picked at the crust with her hammer, and sprinkled me with the prepared water that burnt a little when it sank into my skin.

I got into bed, very carefully, and slept badly. Eventually, of course, they discharged me from the hospital and told me I was cured. Instead of the fresh milk, they gave me a good bowl of soup. After the first spoonful, I started screaming and running around because my insides were like a raw wound, gnawed and rotten from all the bad meat I'd eaten off my Christina. I went out into the street, still screaming. The children were just leaving school, and a little boy, half-frightened because I was staring at him, pointed at me and said in a low voice to the others: "He's the pearl." My hands still gleamed with colored flakes – the kind shellfish have inside them . . . and I looked at the children's eyes, a pack of blue and brown eyes which followed me and wouldn't go away, as if they were hanging in midair with nothing around and were only going to their . . . I stopped. My cheek and the middle of my head were all pearly crust, stuck on so well, so firmly wedded to my flesh that the hammer had never been able to break it. And I stood still till the children had gotten tired of looking at me.

Then I climbed to the top of the rocks, outside the village, up above everything, where you can't go any higher, where the sea birds make their nests and where butterflies die in autumn. It was nighttime. And with my heart full of things that twinkled like the stars, I stayed there, watching the sea and the darkness which covered it. A little light still lingered in the west, fading away. And as soon as everything was really dark, from one side of the sea to the other a broad, peaceful avenue appeared, and down that avenue came my Christina with her spout shooting water and I was riding on her back, clutching my plank like before, singing my sailors' hymn. And from where I was on top of the rocks, I heard it perfectly, sung by me down there in the middle of all that water beyond the avenue, on top of my Christina, who was leaving a trail of blood. I finished singing and Christina stopped and I kept still without breathing, as if all of me had vanished into that gaze. And then she and I above her, silently waving, were lost from sight out towards where the sea curves around to go even further out . . .

I sat down on the ground with my legs pulled up, and fell asleep with my arms around my legs and my head on my arms. And I must have been very tired, because I didn't wake up till dawn, with the screeches of birds who don't know how to sing. They came out of the holes in the rocks, all white, in vast flights all together, throwing themselves at the sea like rocks, and then rising again, whizzing by with fish in their beaks which they gave to their little ones. And some, instead of fish, brought branches and tufts of grass to make nests with. I got up, annoyed by the screeching. The sea was smooth like glass, and I started going down towards the village. When I reached the first houses, a filthy old hag came out of her doorway. She threw herself on me, screaming, "You're my husband, you're my husband and you left me . . ." And I swear it wasn't true, because I'd never been in that village, and if I'd ever seen that woman I would have remembered her because her top teeth came down over her lower lip. I gave her a push and she fell to the ground, and I kicked her to one side, carefully because there was a kid watching from a window.

I went back to where they were making up my papers. They were celebrating something – I'm not sure what. Everyone was drinking white wine from little wineglasses. They were standing up, and the one with the mustache saw me right away and came up to me looking like he wasn't in any mood to be bothered. And I saw one with sleevelets, whispering in the ear of another who was bald, and from the movement of his lips I guessed what he was saying: "The pearl." And they all started looking at me, and the one who'd come up to me said again, "Tomorrow." And he walked me to the door, and almost pushed me out, and he kept saying "tomorrow, tomorrow," like a song.

MERCE RODOREDA was born in Barcelona in 1908, at a time when Catalonia was autonomous and its citizens were allowed to speak, write, and study their own language. She published five novels between 1932 and 1937, and then fled to exile in Paris and then Geneva at the end of the Spanish Civil War, when the Catalan culture was brutally suppressed. She did not publish again until 1959. Afterwards, she regularly produced novels and collections of short stories and became a fixture on Catalan best-seller lists. When Franco died, most restrictions on the use of Catalan were lifted, and Rodoreda returned to Barcelona, where she died of cancer in April, 1983.

DAVID H. ROSENTHAL is well-known for his translations from the Catalan. His most recent book is a translation of the 15th century Catalan classic *Tirant lo Blanc*. He is the translator of Rodoreda's novel *The Time of the Doves*, as well as *Modern Catalan Poetry: An Anthology*. He lives in New York City and spends much of the year in Barcelona.